MARKED BY POWER

CECE ROSE AND G. BAILEY

Contents

Marked by Power

CECE ROSE AND G. BAILEY

Copyright © 2017 Cece Rose & G. Bailey

For the flock, because without the flock this book collaboration would never have happened. <3

Prologue

The dim lighting in the room does nothing to hide the predatory look on his face as he stalks around me, moving in a circle. I keep trying to move with him, to keep my eyes on him and my back away, but he's just too quick. He shoots flames to my left, and I jump to my right, narrowly avoiding the hit.

I try to counter with air, calling on my mark. I aim low, hoping to strike him off balance. He blocks my attack with a simple swipe of his hand. A cool jet of water flows from his right hand; he doesn't aim it at me, but at the floor. I stare at him in confusion, when suddenly the water begins to cool and freeze over. I struggle not to slide across it. I lift my left hand and command fire, using fire's heat to melt the ice. The steam creates a wall between us. I try to use it as a screen to attack, but he simply uses his air ability to clear his vision again. I back up a few steps to keep out of reach, but he pounces, crossing the space between us. Within seconds I'm pinned down onto the blue mat by his weight. I struggle to get loose, completely forgetting to use my magic in order to assist me.

"Miss Crowe," he whispers in my ear softly, his deep voice sending shivers right through me.

"Kenzie," I mumble.

"What?" he asks.

"Please call me Kenzie," I whisper.

"Miss Kenzie Crowe," he utters softly, his cool breath against my neck making me shiver.

"Yes?" I whisper, looking up, and catching the heated look in his green eyes.

"You would be dead six times over if I was really trying."

Chapter 1

KENZIE

*T*oday is the first day of the rest of my life, my initiation into the marked academy. I glance around at all the other seventeen-year-olds dressed in traditional white, as we walk across the rocks. Most look excited, a few nervous, and one even looks a little bored, but I'm calm. I'll be happy whether I get one power, eleven, or any of the numbers in-between. I feel a hand slip in mine, and as I look around to see Kelly, I smile at her.

"Aren't you nervous?" Kelly asks.

"Nope. It doesn't matter what happens. I've just got to last three years in this school, and then I'm back to the plan. It's hard to be nervous when you're not invested," I answer softly, aware of the quiet around us, and not wanting my voice to echo in the darkness of night.

"I am," she whispers. "What if I only get one? My

dads will be so disappointed. Mum will be happy with whatever, but those two, they just have so many expectations," she adds. I frown. I know her dads have always been pushing Kelly to be a high achiever, but seeing her worry like this makes me glad that my own fathers only want me to be happy. The three of them have always shown me support in whatever I want to do, and my mum is the same.

"It'll be fine, Kells, I promise," I reply, squeezing her hand tightly. She shoots me a grateful smile, and then her eyes widen as we reach the cave entrance. The entrance is considerably large for a cave and is mostly filled with water, but for a narrow, uneven ledge that runs along one side.

One by one, we file onto the ledge in alphabetical order, walking slowly and carefully across it. Kelly lets go of my hand reluctantly and slips in behind me, walking so close I can feel her breath on my neck. I'm glad her surname follows mine: Crowe and Curwood, I'd hate to think of her doing this part without me.

We follow along the trail until I see the people in front of me seemingly vanish into the wall. I trail my fingers along, waiting for the crack I know is meant to be there. The guy directly in front of me steps to the side and vanishes. I follow his steps and feel my fingers leave the wall, finding the gap. I slip through after him and walk in darkness for a moment, until I see where the narrow gap opens up. Torches line the walls, the flames flickering and casting shadows everywhere. I carry on following behind the guy in front, and I hear Kelly following closely behind. The path opens into a large cavernous space. A serene pool of water lies between us and a grand, golden, double door. The doors are covered in the twelve markings of the marked, six on each. There are three people cloaked in black standing in front of the door. One stands to the side by a gong, holding a long striker. Another stands slightly to the other side, gesturing to us all to file into the room. And one stands in front, a long gold chain hanging around their neck, the master of today's ceremony.

We all file into rows in front of the water. Once side by side again, I feel Kelly's hand slip back into mine. We kneel as instructed and wait for the rest to file in. Once we are all waiting, kneeling patiently, the master of the ceremony steps forward.

"Welcome, new students, to The Marked Academy. One by one your names will be called, and you shall enter the water. The water here is all the way from Ariziadia, and will activate your dormant powers. You are to submerge to receive your marks at the sound of the gong. Once blessed by the water, you shall declare how many markings you received, before passing through the doors. However, if you are not blessed by the water, you must leave immediately. Do you all understand?"

A mixture of affirmative answers and head nods roll across the room as we indicate our understanding. I feel Kelly's hand squeeze mine tighter, the worry of not being blessed clearly getting to her.

"We shall begin," the ceremony master says. I can

feel the tension in the room as everyone stares forward, waiting for the blessings to begin.

"Jacob Addison," the robed figure to the left calls, their deep voice carrying across the otherwise silent room. The guy kneeling on the front row furthest to the left stands and makes his way to the pool of water. His hunched shoulders are the only sign of his concern as he slowly wades through the water till he reaches the centre and stops, nervously looking around. I count my blessings that I'm not first. The pressure of going before everyone else must be overwhelming.

The robed figure to the right bangs the striker against the gong, and Jacob submerges himself in the water, going completely under. We all watch and wait with bated breath for him to rise. After what feels like forever, he emerges, spluttering and his hands patting against several parts of his body. *He must be counting his marks.*

"How many markings?" the deep voice calls.

"Seven," Jacob replies. He looks around and catches the looks of who I assume to be friends, giving them a thumbs up, before wading the rest of the way across the water. He walks up and past the robed figures before slowly pushing the grand-looking door open and stepping through, the door closing softly behind him.

"Joshua Allen," the robed figure calls, wasting no time in continuing.

The next guy stands and makes his way into the water. The gong sounds, he submerges, and then emerges again.

6

"How many markings?" the robed man asks.

"Four," Joshua answers, his voice wavering over the simple word. Without looking back, he crosses through the water and walks up past the robed figures, and leaves through the golden door as the guy before him did.

"How many more people before us?" Kelly whispers to me softly.

"Twenty-two," I whisper back. "Just be glad our surnames don't begin with Z." I shoot a smile at her, which she returns nervously. *247 of us needing to be blessed, I'm glad I'm not the robed guys right now.* Turning my head, I cast my eyes across to the guy sitting at the back at the far right. *Nope. It's him I am glad not to be, his knees will be aching like hell by the time he gets called.*

I turn my attention back to the ceremony, watching each person stand, as they are called and step into the water. They all receive marks; the lowest three and the highest earning ten. The one with ten gets some impressed looks from other students, who are kneeling and waiting. As I watch Liam Cartwright walk through the large doors on the other side of the water, I take a deep breath.

"Mackenzie Crowe."

Despite expecting it, I freeze when my name is called. I wasn't feeling nervous before, but the water suddenly looks so much more daunting. With so many still in here watching, I feel the pressure mount. *What if I only get one?* It doesn't matter so much to me if I don't have powers, but others may think less of me for it, and I have to put up with these people for the next three years.

What if I stand in the water and have nothing, nada. If I'm not marked, what would happen then? It's not as if that is common, but it's been known to happen; I wouldn't be the first. Not marked, not human, but unmarked. The unmarked are born of a marked line, but not deemed worthy of power. The ultimate failure in the eyes of my people.

I gulp as I stand, straightening my shoulders as I walk the short distance to the water. The water is completely still, not a ripple in sight. I dip my toe in first, feeling the cold shoot straight into me, chilling me to my bones. I cast a glance back at Kelly. She shoots me an encouraging smile and mouths something at me, but I can't make out what. I turn back, looking straight at the door ahead, and step into the water.

I wade in until about waist deep and in the centre of the pool. I look up above, the gap in the ceiling of the cave letting the moonlight in. The glow of the full moon is strangely comforting. The gong sounds, and I submerge a second after, letting the icy-cold water cover me, closing my eyes as my head goes under. I feel the chill of the water make me shiver, and I start to wonder how I will know I have been blessed or not, when I feel a burn on my left ankle. *That's one.* Another on my right hip. *That's two.*

Fuck my ribs! I clutch my ribs with my hands as a burn starts there as well. And then suddenly, pain strikes across my body in several places all at once. The water now feels hot, not cold. I pull myself upright, so I'm standing, shaking slightly. I look down at myself and try to make a count of all the marks, using pain as an indicator of the ones below clothing.

Both ankles, both thighs, both hipbones, my ribs, two on my back, both wrists, and I feel a burn on the back of my neck. *Wait, how many is that?* I do a mental count. *Twelve. That's got to be wrong.* I count again. A throat clears drawing my attention to the hooded figures, knowing I need to announce my markings. I try to count again, coming up with the same answer, twelve. *How is that possible?*

"Miss Crowe?"

"Tw-twelve," I stutter quietly.

"I'm sorry?"

"Twelve," I repeat more clearly. "I have twelve marks."

Whispers start around the room. It doesn't take long for the volume to rise, and for it to become shouting. *Twelve marks, it's impossible.*

I can hear people yelling things like "liar," "deceit," and "check her" as I swallow and slowly make my way across the rest of the pool. I stand before the robed elders, waiting for them to allow me to pass and enter The Academy.

One of the figures steps toward me and holds out their hands, palm up, requesting my own. I place my hands in theirs and they turn my hands over and inspect the two markings on my wrists. The symbol of flames on one, and water on the other. They release them and twirl their fingers, asking me to turn around. I do as they say, facing the other students who are waiting for their own initiation to begin. I feel fingers lightly brush my thick, dark hair out of the way and then trace over the marking on my neck. I shiver from the gentleness of the touch.

"I don't need to see anymore," the man's voice says quietly. "This is the twelfth marking on your neck. I've never seen anyone wear this mark. I believe what you say is true."

I release a breath I didn't realise I'd been holding. *At least, he isn't going to make me strip in front of most of my classmates on the first day. Now, that would have been embarrassing.*

"Continue into the school, Miss Crowe. We will speak with you once the ceremony is over," he says it softly, so the words don't carry.

I nod my head and slip past him, eager to get away from all the eyes watching me. I reach the large door and push, it opens far more easily than I'd expected. I walk through and allow the door to close behind me, cutting off the stares. Just as the door is about to close, I hear them call Kelly's name.

Chapter 2

KENZIE

_T_welve marks. I have twelve marks, and the twelve powers that go with them. _How did this happen?_ I've never heard of anyone having twelve marks before. The highest number of marks I've heard about was a guy who got eleven last year. He was a hero around my community for months; everyone was talking about him. I try not to think of anything more and let my mind circle around the facts, as I walk up the dozens of high steps to another pair of big doors. I push open the doors to a large hallway, and I shut them behind me. Shivering from the cold, as my wet dress sticks to me, my long hair drips water onto the floor. Every drop echoes as it hits the ground in the otherwise silent hallway. I move quietly down the corridor, hating how my shoes sound squishy against the shiny, pristine floor.

"Here," a woman says, making me jump as she

steps out of the shadows at the side of the hallway. I can't see what she looks like as she has a black cloak on, and the large hood is covering her face. She hands me a folded, black cloak much like the one she is wearing, and I happily take it from her as I'm freezing.

I pull the cloak around my shoulders and pull the hood up, still cold but not shivering as badly now that I'm under the thick material. The woman steps back, mixing into the shadows again. *Probably hiding to freak the new students out for fun; I know I would.*

The corridor is surprisingly modern, nothing like I would expect an ancient manor on an island to look like. Modern chandeliers hang from the ceiling above me, casting a soft glow. The white walls are pristine and dark-wood floors look newly polished. The walls are covered in a mixture of ancient artifacts. There is everything from a giant sword, to what I'm guessing is a fish hook. There is also a strange looking, massive claw in a glass box. *What could that be from?* All along the wall are weapons, paintings, and various other things. I'd have to come take a better look at the other objects some time.

I've seen photos of this island before. I know it's located just off the coast of Scotland, and that it looks like a wreck from the outside. I'm sure that's some kind of ruse to keep humans out, as well as having the protection wards spelled into the island by the first of the marked to settle here.

I keep walking towards the open doors at the end of the corridor. There are massive, dark-wood stairs on either side going up to the next level, and when I look up, the stairs wind all the way up to the top of the manor. At the top, is a glass dome where I can see the stormy, grey skies outside. There must be at least five levels from what I can see.

I'm just about to go through the large doors, when I stop as I hear doors open behind me. I turn to see Kelly walking in, and she shakes her head at me as our eyes meet. Even from this distance, I can see her eyes are filled with tears. Her dress is soaking wet, clinging to her small frame and wet, blonde hair is plastered against the sides of her face.

"Please move into the hall," a man says from behind me in a sharp voice. Turning I see a guy not much older than me holding the door open.

"But, can't I just wait for my friend?" I ask as I turn to look at him.

He shakes his head. "Move on," the man says, his tone leaving no room for argument. I glance once more at my friend before turning and walking into the hall.

The room is massive, and filled with students all dressed in black robes sitting down on chairs located on either side of the room. The hall has dozens of little balls of glass lights hanging from the ceiling, they are all a mixture of yellows and reds. I know they aren't any kind of marked magic, but they have a certain magical effect on the room.

The floor is the same dark wood as the corridor, and the walls are gold and white panels. The twelve marks are drawn on each section of the walls that are gold, six on each side like the doors. My eyes glance at the twelfth mark, seeing it painted in black against the gold.

The twelfth mark looks like a sphere, with an arrow going through it. The arrow splits the sphere in half. Unless my new power is cutting things in half, the mark is no help in figuring out what the power is. *No wonder nobody has figured it out before.*

A throat clears, and I pick up my pace, realising how slowly I'm moving due to gaping at the room around me. There is a gold, marked path in the middle of the students for the new entrants to walk down. I can see the other new students at the front of the hall as I get closer, behind them are three large, glass windows that overlook the rough sea. I can see the crashing waves in the water from here.

I walk faster down the middle of the students, not glancing at anyone, but I feel their stares on me. The room is so quiet that I can hear my every footstep in my wet shoes. I bite my tongue softly, feeling heat flush to my cheeks. I try and force myself not to think about the fact there are so many students here, and soon, every single one of them will know I have all twelve marks. At the end of the path, is a small stage where all the new students are sitting on seats. I lift my cloak and dress as I walk up the few steps, and I take the next empty seat in the line. When I sit down, my eyes go straight to Kelly who has just walked in. I watch her like everyone else as she wipes her eyes and quickly walks to the stage. She takes the seat next to me and I slide my hand into hers.

"How many marks?" I ask softly. She shakes her

head, and I know that's not a good sign. *I knew her tears could only be for one reason.*

"It doesn't matter," I tell her, and her blue eyes look up at me.

"Says you, who got twelve marks," she replies sarcastically, forgoing the whisper. Her voice echoes around the quiet room. I cringe from the volume, but I know she didn't mean it. She's just worried about her dads' reaction to her own marks.

I realise that the other students must have heard as the whispers start instantly. I feel myself getting warm from all the eyes on me. *Great, well everyone knows now.* I lift my eyes to the crowd of students, and everyone is staring with shocked and disbelieving faces.

"Shit, I'm sorry, Kenzie. I got two marks, just two," Kelly says quietly, pulling my attention from the crowd. I squeeze her hand. I go to tell her that it will be okay, when I see three robed figures walking towards us.

They are all different heights, and their faces are hidden under their different-coloured cloaks, but I know who they are from the symbols on their clothing, the three headmasters of the school. I remember my older brother telling me about them, about how strict they all are, about how everyone in the school is afraid of their power, including the other teachers. The three of them stop in front of us on the stage, and the one with the green cloak speaks, his voice loud and deep.

"We welcome our new marked to our academy," the man in the green says and takes a pause as everyone claps.

"Every year we welcome our new marked, the new generation to carry on our gifts. We will talk to every student privately and assign them their student guides for the first year as the others continue to come in," the red cloaked man adds. I watch as he pulls out a tablet and switches it on.

"Mackenzie Crowe, please come with me," the man in the green cloak says, turning to face me, but I still can't see his face under the hood.

"Mackenzie's guide will be Easton Black," the man in the red cloak says, as he reads from a list from his large tablet. I'm too in shock from hearing that familiar name to question why I'm going first, instead of the others who were sitting waiting.

My eyes find a very familiar pair in the first two rows of students, as East stands up and pulls his hood down. Hazel eyes and soft-looking brown hair with blond highlights; his hair is messy and long, but pulled away from his face. He doesn't need to do much to his hair, and it still looks ridiculously gorgeous, as always. His lips turn up into a sexy smile that shows off the dimples I remember so fondly.

My brother's best friend, Easton Black, was always around when we were younger. He is also the boy I've had a crush on since I was thirteen, and he has never noticed me at all.

He looks every bit as sexy as I remember.

"Sexy East is your guide," Kelly whispers, and I give her a look that says 'shut up', and she smiles for a second. I haven't seen him in two years, not since he came here. Easton walks over to me at the same time I stand up. Neither of us speaks as we follow the man in the green cloak out of the room through a door near the stage. We come into another corridor with four wooden doors. The man opens the first door to the left and walks in.

"Please wait outside, Mr. Black," the man says and Easton nods, moving to stand near the wall, but his eyes stay on mine.

"Good luck, Kenzie," Easton says, his first words to me. Easton's voice is made for seduction. Growing up, he always had a way with girls because of his good looks and deep voice. His voice sends shivers through me that I can't blame on being cold.

I walk into the small room and pull the door shut behind me. The room has a big, wooden desk and two seats on each side. There are two small bookcases full of books and some green curtains on the small window in the room. I take my seat, as the cloaked man pulls his hood down and moves to his chair behind the desk. The man is older than I expected from his voice, with short, grey hair and a full, grey beard. I would guess his age at around fifty.

"I'm Mr. Lockhart, one of the three headteachers at the academy. Mr. Daniels told me of your marks that you received today. I believe he saw the twelfth?" he says.

"Yes," I say, and he nods at me.

"May I see it?" he asks, already standing up, leaving me with not much choice but to show him the mark as he walks around the desk.

"Sure," I reply, lifting my hair. Mr. Lockhart

moves behind my chair, and the room seems to stay still for a long time as he stares at my mark. I wait quietly until he moves back to his seat and leans back in shock.

"I am lost for words, Miss Crowe. I'm sure you know that no marked has been gifted with the twelfth mark in years. The only reason we know it exists, is because it is in the Book of Marks," he says. I remember one of my dads telling me about the Book of Marks; a large book bound in leather and printed on vellum. A book with just twelve thick pages, each with a different mark on it. The book is thousands of years old, and it's believed that it came from Ariziadia, like the water in the cave under the academy.

"Does the book say what the mark does? What my power is?" I ask him, but I think I know the answer.

"Unfortunately, the book does not tell us what the powers of the marks are. It only shows us the design," he answers, picking up his glasses from the table. I don't say a word as he opens a book and pulls out a blank timetable. He quickly pencils in classes across the week. "These are your eleven classes. I have split them over the course of the week for you, but I'm afraid you will not get much time off other than Sunday."

"Eleven classes?" I say, my voice a mixture of anger and disbelief. I can't do that many. I'm suddenly wishing I only got one mark. At least, I'd only have to take one class.

"Yes, you will need to take all eleven. We will split them into two classes a day in the week and just one on Saturday," he says writing down a copy of this unfair plan of his on some paper in front of him. "I'm afraid you will not get to pick any elective classes either, due to already having to take all eleven of the mark classes."

"That's—" I start to say, but he cuts me off.

"Necessary for you to learn how to control all your powers. Having so many mark powers will be a challenge for you, and you do not want to lose control," he tells me.

I think on the stories I've heard about powerful marked that lost control . . . they always ended up dead. The bedtime stories for marked children were never pretty, but neither were the stories in the book of human fairy tales aunt Laura gave me. The only difference is, our bedtime stories were true.

"How long are each of the classes?" I ask, dreading the answer.

"Three and a half hours," he answers. I groan, sliding down in my seat.

You have got to be kidding me.

Chapter 3

KENZIE

I let my towel drop and gaze at my reflection in the full-length mirror, more specifically at the markings that now cover my body. I've always wondered where my markings would appear, how many I'd have, and what they'd look like on my skin. I can't help but think of them being more than just pretty ink on my skin. The meaning behind all of the symbols is clear. From the fire and water symbols on my wrists, to the earth and air symbols on my ankles. On my thighs on one side is pain, and on the other is healing. My hip bones, one is technomancy, the other transmutation. On my ribs is the symbol for protection, right under my heart on the left side.

I turn around and look over my shoulder, looking at the symbols on my back. Divination near the top, spirit on the base of my spine. Mark number twelve is on my neck, the one nobody knows about; I'm not even sure what to call it. I sigh and pick my towel up from the floor, wrapping it around myself. A knock hits the door, startling me, so I almost drop my towel again.

"Kenzie?" I hear Kelly's soft-spoken voice calling.

"Yeah?"

"Are you gonna take all day? I wanted a shower and breakfast starts in ten minutes." I cast a guilty look between the shower and the door. She'd have luck getting any more hot water out of there.

"Can you have one later? I'm almost done, but I wanna go get food now. I'm starving," I call back through the door. I can see her eyes rolling in my mind as she sighs loudly and dramatically.

"Fine, Kenzie. But, if I get sat next to a hottie, and he thinks I'm a weird, non-showering hobo, I'm blaming you."

"Fair," I call back. I quickly pull on some clothes and towel dry my wet hair, forgoing makeup. I make my way back out into the room where Kelly is just brushing her own hair, already dressed and ready to go. She's looking stylishly dressed, and her makeup is perfectly done. *Non-showering hobo my ass.*

"You only said you wanted a shower to hurry me up, didn't you," I accuse.

"Maybe . . . but it worked, right?" she replies with a smirk, clearly much cheerier today.

"What classes do you have today?" I ask, slipping my shoes on.

"Just the one. I haven't had the chance to sign up for electives yet, and I only have two required classes," she says, her voice losing its previously cheery tone.

"Hey, it's okay, at least you can pick some fun electives! I've got eleven classes of boring," I answer.

"Yeah, I guess," she says, her eyes not meeting mine.

"Well, you can just pick whatever electives the hot guys sign up for, is that not a great idea? Suss out your boyfriend options early?"

"Ugh, I don't think I'll find a boyfriend here, Kenzie. Who would want me, a weak two-powered marked?"

I roll my eyes. Pity parties were not going to help her out of this funk. "Kelly, you're beautiful, kind, smart, and have boobs for days," I say gesturing to her sizeable chest area. "I'm sure you will have no troubles finding as many boyfriends as you'd like." She smiles deviously.

"What if I wanted ten?" she asks, the grin growing wider.

"Then, you get yourself ten. Although, I don't know what you'd do with ten . . . what would they do . . . just stand around you in a giant circle?" I wink at her, and then pull a face. Her eyes widen, and her mouth drops open as she picks up on my undertone.

"Kenzie!" she spits out.

"What? What do you think marked woman are doing with their multiple husbands behind closed doors, playing scrabble?" I chuckle at her mortified expression. Then her expression turns calculating, a smile takes over her face.

"I have two dads, you had four. Whose mum had a circle going?" she laughs, as my own face mirrors her previous mortified look. *Not what I want to picture.* I shudder.

"Okay, okay. That's enough talk about man circles for now."

"Yes! Does that mean breakfast?" she asks, clearly as excited by the prospect of food as I am.

"Let's pray there is bacon," I mumble back.

We make our way out of our room, locking it behind us. I'm so glad I have Kelly as my roommate. It would have sucked to have been stuck with some bitch for three years. Instead, I get my best friend. We race down the steps of the dorm building and out into the chilly, morning air. I instantly regret forgoing a jacket. *Hell, even one of the stupid ceremony robes would be great right now. It's fucking freezing.*

We make our way through the courtyard and towards the main building, where the dining hall is located. Breakfast is served between 7:30am-9:30am daily, and we were going to be some of the first there at this rate, but fuck it, I'm starving. Neither of us could bring ourselves to eat last night, so it only makes sense we're both eager to make our way to breakfast this morning. We walk through the already open front doors, and turn left towards the dining hall. A quick walk down a corridor, and we're there.

There are tables set to one side covered in hot plates with food on them, and trays, plates, and cutlery at the start. Despite being here bright and early, there is already a line. We walk across the room and join the orderly queue. I'm about to say something when I notice a petite, blonde girl, sashay across the room, and directly to the front of the queue. At just a look from the girl, the guy in the front just backs away and lets her in without a word.

"Oh no," I mutter, giving Kelly the look.

"Guess we spotted the bitchy girl nice and early," Kelly mutters.

"Hey, let's not judge too quickly. Maybe she just has an aversion to queuing. I say we suss her out first," I reply.

Hearing a deep, throaty chuckle behind me, I turn around to spot Easton standing there. His messy hair looking like he just woke up perfect.

"Hey, East," I say softly, trying not to drool. Men shouldn't be that attractive. Kelly's eyes widen, and she turns around, too. Every girl crushed on Easton back in our small town, Kelly included. Although, I'd wager my crush was far more intense and embarrassing. The fact he was always in my house didn't help.

"She is," he says simply, breaking my train of thought.

"Who is what?" I ask confused.

"The bitchy girl. That girl has claws," he answers.

"I knew it," Kelly mutters.

"Really, what did she do to you?" I ask.

"She asked me out," he answers, smirking.

"And, that makes her a bitch?"

"No. But, when I said no, she decided to tell the girl I used to be interested in, that I was sleeping with her. Stella is just like that. If you're not serving her needs, your only use to her is for a fuck, or she will make your life hell." He laughs, but it's hollow. I frown, both mad at Stella for her actions, and super happy that it seems like Easton doesn't currently have a girlfriend. *What can I say? I'm petty like that.*

We reach the front of the queue, and I waste no time piling my plate with food. *Fuck, I'm starving.* I catch a bemused look on Easton's face as I turn to find a table.

"What?" I ask him.

"You're gonna eat all of that?" he questions.

"Maybe seconds too, ya know, if I feel like it."

"You never used to eat that much as a kid," he says.

"Like you ever noticed me," I mumble.

"Should we sit over there," Kelly interrupts, gesturing to the furthest table, the one out of the way of everyone else. *Typical Kelly.*

"No, we're gonna sit there," I answer, nodding my head in the direction of the table at the centre of the room.

"What?" Kelly snaps in shock.

"Come on, Kells," I say in my most cheery voice. *I will not let her hide herself away.* We take seats around the table, and I'm pleasantly surprised when Easton joins us.

"What classes have you girls got today?" he asks around a mouthful of toast.

"Divination, and fire," I answer.

"Just Divination for me," Kelly answers.

His eyes roll at the mention of Divination.

"I still don't know why that's counted as a power, it's not like anyone ever sees anything useful. There are a few people who get good at seeing the past, but so few actually have a good skill at seeing the future. Even when they do, it's never clear or predictable. I don't get why they teach it as a class," he says. I see a frown take over Kelly's face. *Fuck's sake. Did he have to put his foot in it?*

"It's a power, the same as any other. It's a hard one to master is all. I'm sure Kells will kill it, though. You've always been good at guessing what's going to happen when we watch films and stuff." I shoot her a smile. "I bet that was your powers shining through early."

"Yeah, whatever," she mutters, huffing. "So long as I can actually see something. I'm more interested in my healing class later this week, to be honest," she adds.

"See now, healing, that's one of the best powers. It may not be cool or flashy, but it's certainly one of the most useful. Healing people is good." I roll my eyes at East's mansplaining. Like we don't already know that.

"It's a good thing you're pretty, East," I tease, flicking some of my orange juice at him.

"Huh?"

"Nothing," I chime in a cheery tone. He narrows his eyes and opens his mouth to say something, when two guys suddenly sit on either side of him. I blink my eyes, thinking I must be seeing double, when it hits me, they're twins. *Hot twins at that.* They both have short, blond hair, which is styled similarly and big, muscular bodies. The twin on the right has a clean-shaven jaw, and the other has a slight five o'clock shadow.

"And, how do you know Easton here?" one of them asks, slamming his tray down onto the table.

"Yeah, Easton doesn't often bring pretty girls to join us for meals," the other adds, placing his own tray on the table.

"She's Ryan's sister," Easton answers.

"Really?" they both ask at once.

"She looks nothing like him," the one on the left says.

"A good thing at that, she doesn't," the other on the right adds.

"Are you calling my big brother ugly?" I snap, and glare at them both. They both look taken aback and start to apologise.

I lose my stern face and smile. "Good, he is an ugly fucker," I tease.

They're both stunned into silence for a moment, before both relaxing and laughing. East smiles at me. "You have to lower your humour to the basics around these two, Kenzie. Sarcasm is above their level of understanding."

"Shut up," leftie snaps.

"We're much funnier than you, pretty boy," the one on the right adds. East just twirls his hand in a circle by his head. *Cuckoo.* His sentiments on the matter are clear.

CECE ROSE AND G. BAILEY

"I'm Mackenzie, that's Kelly," I say, properly introducing us.

"I'm Locke," leftie introduces himself, the one with the five o'clock shadow.

"And, I'm Logan," righty adds.

"And, if you didn't already guess," leftie begins.

"We're twins," righty finishes.

"Nice to meet you both. I'm guessing you're in the year above then?" I ask, hedging a guess.

"Yup, second years now," Locke says.

"East is in his final year, though," Logan adds.

"I knew that. He's a year younger than my brother," I reply and eat some more of my food, I look at the twins trying to work out an easier way to tell them apart. Locke's hair is slightly longer, and a little messier than his twin's.

"Did you hear about that chick with twelve marks?" Locke asks, and I freeze with a piece of bacon in my mouth.

"Yeah, I mean, that's a shit-load of powers, but no one thinks she will last a week without killing herself accidently," Logan says.

"Shut it, Logan," East snaps, whacking his arm, and I slide my chair out as I stand up.

"Kenzie," East starts, and I wave a hand.

"It was me that got all twelve, and I have a class to get to," I say, and both the twins lean back in their chairs in shock. I can't stop my eyes tracing over their blue shirts and the muscles that I can see on their arms.

"Let's go, the library is next door to your class by

the looks of it, and I have to pick my electives," Kelly says, standing up with me.

"Wait, I'm your guide, and I'm meant to show you to your classes for the first week," East says.

"I don't need your help," I reply and turn around before he can say anything. We both walk out, and I look back to see East staring at me. His face is a mixture of concern and something else.

Like he is seeing me for the first time.

Chapter 4
EASTON

"*R*yan's sister has twelve marks? The fucker must be jealous with his seven," Locke says, and I narrow my eyes at him.

"Ry asked me to watch her for him. I can't do that if you fucking scare her away, man," I say, and he shrugs with a grin. I look back at the doors where Kenzie is leaving, and she looks back, her bright-blue eyes staring straight through me. I run my eyes down her sexy as fuck body. *Has Kenzie always been this hot?*

I can't remember her looking like this. I remember her two years ago, with her short, black hair and baggy clothes. This Kenzie has a thin waist that shapes up to an impressive chest shown off in her tight clothes. When Kenzie turns, her long, black hair moves around her, and I know I have an issue. I'm not looking at her like I should be: like she is a friend. No,

I can't stop looking at her ass just before the door shuts behind her.

When I agreed to watch over my best friend's little sister, I remembered the teenage girl that followed us around. Not this Kenzie, she is something else entirely.

"Fuck," I mutter, pushing my plate away and leaning back in my seat. I place my hands on the back of my neck and look up at the ceiling.

"You're thinking about how sexy of an ass Kenzie has, too?" Logan says, and I have to resist the urge to punch him as I look at him. These fuckers are annoying, but I like them. We fight well together, and when I had a lot of shit with my parents going on, they helped.

"She is Ryan's sister," I say, forcing myself to remember us growing up together and not how her ass looked in those jeans. Kenzie was always around when I hung out with Ry.

"And? He isn't here," he says and knocks my shoulder. My phone starts ringing, stopping me from replying to the cheeky fucker. He damn well knows Ryan would kick all our asses if we touched Kenzie. I pull my phone out and accept the unknown number's call.

"Hey, shitface, how's my sister?" Ryan says as a hello. I rub my hand over my face. *It's like he finally can use his divination power or some shit.*

"Kenzie got twelve marks, but otherwise is fine," I say, and there is silence on the other side of the phone for a long time.

"Fucking hell. Kennie got twelve?" Ry shouts

down the phone, eventually. I think we are as fucking shocked as he is. The twins didn't know because they bailed on the ceremony yesterday, but I'm certain most of the school knows by now.

"Yeah, I know, man," I say.

"You still keeping your promise?" he asks.

"Yeah, man. I'll keep an eye on Kenzie. I'm her student guide, anyway," I say, ignoring the fact she walked off without me already. She used to follow me around back home, and now, she comes here and just walks away. Shaking her perfect ass as she goes.

"Yeah, he wants a guide into her fucking knickers," Locke says and laughs with Logan. I glare at them both as Ry tells me about his new job. So glad he didn't overhear that. Such fuckers.

"So, the job is good?" I ask.

"Yeah, man, it's what I was meant to be doing, you know?" he says. Ry got the perfect job straight out of the academy. He works for our council by finding rogue marked and bringing them to justice. There is a group who regularly use their powers against humans, breaking one of the most important laws we have.

"Caught any yet?" I ask, and he laughs.

"Nah, but we have a big mission next week. I can't tell you more, man, but it's only a year until you join me," he says. I'm a seven like Ry, and my main power is transfiguration, so I would be good for hunting. Ry is good at air.

"I've got to go," I say, when I hear the bell sound. We have five minutes until the second bell goes, marking the start of class.

"I owe you, and tell Kenz to answer her damn phone," he says, and I laugh.

"She is always losing that thing or at least, she used to," I reply. We both say later before I put my phone away and stand up.

"You off to water class?" Locke asks, and I nod.

"Coming?" I ask Logan. The twins may look alike, but they are opposite in their powers. Locke is good with water and healing. Logan is good with fire and pain. They both have seven marks, but they are strong. The fuckers are amazing when they team up, their powers complementing each other.

"Yes, let's go," Locke says and stands up stretching.

I glance once more at my phone, wondering if it's easier to just stay away from Kenzie. Only, the thought of her being alone to deal with twelve powers doesn't sit well with me. I will find her later and patch things up. She needs her student guide, anyway, and I have a promise to keep.

Chapter 5

KENZIE

"*S*hit, I should have let East show us where to go," I say, casting my eyes around the corridor, not a clue where we are meant to be.

"Oh, I have that academy app they told us to download. There must be a map," Kelly replies, stopping in the corridor to pull her phone from her coat pocket. *Shit, I don't even know where I put mine last night.* I didn't even know there was an app to begin with.

I lean over her shoulder and watch her switch on the Academy app and find the map they have on there. One of the best things about this academy is the Technomancy students. My brother always said the Wi-Fi is perfect here, and that the whole place is wired up.

"Ah, it's down here," she says as the app finds where we are, and an icon hovers above the classroom

I need and the library next-door to it. People push past us, in a rush to get to classes like we are, and I know we are going to be late when I hear a second bell ring. We searched the entire second floor before realising that it's the third floor we needed. *This place is a maze.*

"See you later," I mumble as we get to my room and Kelly waves at me.

"Good luck," she replies cheerily, and I take a deep breath before opening the door to my classroom. I walk in, and the room goes silent, all of the students are here by the looks of it, and the teacher gives me a look of disgust.

"Miss Crowe, I assume?" she asks and crosses her arms. *Holy smokes, this teacher is intimidating.* She has long, shiny, red hair, bright-green eyes, and the body of a supermodel. I want to say it looks fake, but it's likely the bitch was just born that way.

"Yes, sorry I'm late. I got lost," I answer.

She tuts as she looks me over. "Having twelve marks does not mean you will be treated specially in this academy. I do not care for your excuses, now take a seat, Miss Crowe," she says. Snickers of laughter and whispering follow her words from the other students. I hold in the urge to call her a bitch.

"*Sorry again,*" I say, not bothering to hold in my sarcastic tone. I don't wait for a reply and walk down the middle aisle of the row of desks. I find an empty desk two rows in and take a seat.

"Welcome, new students, to your first fire class. I'm Miss Tinder," she says, introducing herself. *Most guys would be happy if they swiped left on the Tinder app and found her.* "In this class, we will study fire and how to control it. Fire can be many things, but it is known for being uncontrollable," she explains, and I watch as she holds her hands out flat in front of her, and two balls of orange flames appear. "Except that is the very job of the fire marked. We must control it, otherwise fire can destroy," she adds, closing her hands slowly. I watch as the balls of fire get smaller as she does, and then, they disappear altogether. I've seen one of my dads do the same thing. He is strong with his fire, despite having only four marks.

"We first must find out how strong you are with your fire. Some may not be very good, and others will find fire to be their strongest power," she explains. "So, class, I want all of you to step outside and one by one, we will test your powers. Once I have an idea of your personal strength, I can assign you partners that are near your level," she says, and everyone stands up. I move outside with the rest, and Miss Tinder comes outside with us. She calls the first person in, a guy standing close to the door.

I watch five students go in and out, before she comes out and says my name. I follow her back into the classroom and move to stand in front of her.

"Call your fire," she says, not giving any other explanation. I think back to how my one dad said he called his marks. He said you just imagine the mark in your mind. I hold both my hands out and imagine the fire mark the best I can. The mark looks like a flame, with black wavy lines in the middle.

I open my eyes to see a large ball of blue fire in my hands, the ball is getting bigger and bigger. I do the first thing I can think of and drop it. I expected it to disappear, but it doesn't. Fucking hell, it only gets bigger as I jump back.

"Stop," Miss Tinder says, but it's too late. The fire ball rolls around the room, getting bigger, and I try to call it back to no avail. *I know, maybe I can use air to put it out.*

I call my air mark the same way as I did the fire, picturing the mark in my head and calling on it. The next thing I'm aware of, is the feeling of myself flying across the room and slamming into the wall. I hear Miss Tinder shouting, and as I look up, the whole room is on fire.

What was once the ball of fire seemsto have split into five towers of flames, they swirl like tornados and are setting everything on fire as they move. One of the fire tornados swirls its way towards me, and I hold my hands up, begging my air mark to stop this. The tornado just spreads in a long wall of fire, which still keeps moving closer to me. I cough on the smoke, looking around for any way out, but I can't see one. There are no windows in here, and the door is on the other side of the room.

I cough some more, and wipe my eyes as they start watering from the smoke. Water. I can use water. I go to call on my mark, when a guy walks through the flames. Just fucking walks through them. He's tall, with short, black hair, and a serious expression as he looks down at me. The guy looks about my age, and he is gorgeous. With his built body and dark, almost-black eyes, he's captivating. He spreads his arms wide and water shoots out of his hands in streams. The streams shoot around the room like a wave, putting out all the fire. The guy claps his hands, the water stops and just falls to the floor. *That was impressive.*

"Good job, Crowe," the man says with a disgusted look, as he wipes the ash from his leather jacket. I watch as he walks out of the classroom, leaving the door open. *Why did he have to open that sexy mouth of his and ruin the pretty image?*

I pull myself to my feet, just in time to see Miss Tinder come back into the classroom. Her hair is burnt off on one side, and if looks could kill, I would surely be dead right now. The rage has turned her pretty face ugly more than missing some hair ever could.

"Get to the headteachers office, now!" she shrieks. *Oh shit.* I go to leave the room, when I realise I have no damn idea where to go. I turn back to face her and flinch at the expression on her face.

"Err . . . where is that exactly?" I mumble.

"Are you completely incompetent? Use your phone app like every other new student does!"

"But I —"

"Not buts! Get to the headmasters' office, now!" she snaps.

"Okay," I mumble, rushing from the classroom. I notice the guy who walked through the flames leaning against a wall outside.

"Headmasters office?" I ask. He smirks and points

38

left. "Thanks!" I quickly dart in that direction, praying I can find the place.

I rush down several corridors, looking at every door for sign of an office. I poke my head down every corridor I walk by. After about half an hour of searching, I come to realise I've been had. The headmasters' office is definitely not this way. *What an asshole.* I smack my fist against a wall in frustration.

"God damn it!" I curse, cradling my hand. *Fuck that hurt. Stupid wall.*

"Miss Crowe?" a deep voice calls from behind me, the same voice I remember from the initiation ceremony. I turn around and try to lift my jaw from the floor. *Where the fuck are they hiring teachers here from, Hollywood? Runways?* I try not to stare, but find myself ultimately failing.

He looks far too young to be a teacher, so I assume he must be in his early twenties. His green eyes are bright and alluring, and framed by glasses that only seem to add to his hot teacher vibe. His smart, but laidback style clothing does nothing to hide the killer body he has. His shirt is tight against his body, showing off every inch of his hotness. His hair is brown and messy, in a way that just demands you run your hands through it. I can almost picture how soft it would be.

"Miss Crowe?" he asks again, pulling me from my inspection.

"Huh?"

"I asked, is your hand okay?" he says softly, his voice filled with concern.

"Um, yeah, it's fine," I mumble, lifting my hand out, and wriggling my fingers for good measure. I wince. *Okay, maybe not so fine.*

"Here, let me help," he says, as he takes my hand in his. His hands are gentle as he holds my injured hand in both of his, for a moment there is nothing, and then I feel his hands begin to warm. They heat up until they feel almost burning hot, he then releases my hand. I pull back and try wriggling my fingers again tentatively. When no pain comes, I wriggle them more, still nothing. I feel flutters in my stomach that have nothing to do with the magic he just used to heal me.

"Thank you," I say, looking up and meeting his deep-green eyes.

"You're welcome, Miss Crowe. I believe you are meant to be in class right now, are you not?" he asks.

"Um . . . yeah. I kind of got sent to the headmasters' office, but I have no idea where that is, if I'm honest," I explain.

"Have you not downloaded the Academy app?" he asks.

"Well, the thing is, I have no idea where my phone is, so no. I'm not really a tech-friendly person. Tech kind of hates me. Ironic considering that I apparently have the technomancy power as well. I would have never believed that I would get that mark," I reply. He smiles at me, and it takes everything I have not to fucking swoon. *Damn.*

"I'll show you where the office is, come with me," he offers, still smiling. I nod my head and follow him, he slows down to match my pace. I look up at him

40

from his side profile. *He's just as damn hot from this angle too!* I can feel my heart slamming against my chest as he walks closely beside me. *Damn. They didn't make my teachers like this in the human school I went to, that's for sure.* I draw my eyes away from him and will my heart to slow down its beats.

Teacher or not, he is way too unattainable for me, anyway.

Chapter 6

KENZIE

*S*itting on a small, uncomfortable chair across from two of the three headmasters, is not how I wanted to start off my school year here.

"Mr. Daniels, thank you so much for showing Mackenzie to our office," one of the headmasters says. He's dressed in all black: black trousers, black tie, black shirt. It stands out in complete contrast to his fair skin and white-blond hair.

"Yes, that will be all," the other, Mr. Lockhart, adds adjusting his blue tie.

"Actually, I'd like to stay. If that would be acceptable?" he asks, taking up a position sitting on the edge of a low filing cabinet, clearly not waiting for an answer.

"Yes, yes, that will be fine. Now, Mackenzie, it appears you lost control of your fire power in your lesson today?" His beady eyes narrow on me, and I feel myself squirm in my seat.

"But, sirs, it was my first lesson, it was just an accident," I mumble. I try to look anywhere but at the headteacher dressed in black. His beady eyes are giving me the creeps.

"It was many students' first lesson today, and yet, they did not set fire to their classrooms," he replies.

Yeah, but they didn't have a teacher that gave them no frickin instruction. I bite my lip to keep in my retort, instead casting my eyes downward.

"Mr. Layan, we have had other students lose control in the past, and I remember one who destroyed the swimming pool. I believe all Miss Crowe needs is training," Mr. Daniels says, interrupting whatever Mr. Layan was going to say next. *They have a frickin swimming pool here?*

"That may be true, but still, this is not acceptable," he says, his tone frustrated that Mr. Daniels is sticking up for me. Even I don't really understand why he is.

"Of course not," Mr. Daniels says, his voice placating as he watches me closely. Mr. Lockhart is watching me, too, but doesn't say a word. Just sits, with his hands folded on his lap.

"We have no other option than to give you detention, where I hope to see an improvement on your powers in six months," Mr. Layan says. I get the feeling out of the three of the headmasters, he is the one with the most power over the school.

"Six months?" I ask, shocked. That's seriously steep

for a little mistake on the first day. *Just, you know, accidently making fire tornadoes in your first class must happen all the time.* I barely hold in a laugh at that thought.

"Yes. We would usually suspend a student for an incident like this, but we will let it pass this once," he replies, and looks to Mr. Lockhart, who nods his agreement.

"Why?" I ask, my voice dripping with suspicion. I have a feeling it's because of my twelfth mark, and that they want to know what it does. *Don't we all?* I know I shouldn't have said anything when he glares at me, not answering.

"Mr. Daniels, you will take over detention every Sunday. Hopefully, you can teach Miss Crowe some control over her powers," Mr. Lockhart says, finally speaking, but it's not to me. *Frickin great, the one day I have off, and I'm going to be in detention.*

"I would be happy to," Mr. Daniels responds, and I look over at him, his warm eyes watching me closely, and his lips turn up in a smirk. *Maybe detention wouldn't be so bad? I mean, at least there is a good view guaranteed.* He stands up and walks to the door, holding it open for me.

"Bye," I say to them, and they nod, one after the other. It's a little creepy. I walk out of the room and wait for Mr. Daniels to close the door behind me.

"I'm afraid we have missed lunch while we waited for the headmasters to get here. What class do you have this afternoon?" he asks me.

"Divination," I say.

"That's on the top floor, come on," he replies,

nodding his head and walking down the corridor. I catch up and walk by his side. There are a few students rushing around, they don't look our way as they hurry to their classes.

"Tell me what really happened in fire class today, Miss Crowe," he asks me, his voice soft, but there's an undertone of concern in it that I pick up on. *He probably thinks I'm mad after seeing me punch a wall earlier.*

"Why do you think anything happened other than me setting fire to a classroom?" I ask, and he smiles down at me as we get to the staircase.

"Just a hunch," he says, but there's a note of humour in his tone. I follow him up the first staircase, and then we go up the next.

"Miss Tinder didn't explain how to stop my power. I imagined a ball of flames like she asked, and then dropped it, thinking it would go out. I then tried to use air to put it out, but that only made fire tornados—" I stop blabbering on when I trip up a step, and his arm catches me, pulling me close to his chest as he stops me from falling. *Holy smokes, this teacher is way too attractive up close.* I can see the deep-green of his eyes behind his glasses and the smooth, faultless skin. *How is he this friggin attractive and my teacher, a teacher I can't just kiss?*

"Careful, Miss Crowe," he says in a whisper, his arm still around my waist. The sound of a bell ringing startles him, making him step back and clear his throat. We carry on walking as he speaks, and we get to the next set of stairs.

"Never use air to put out fire. It only feeds it. Water would have been ideal," he explains.

"I was going to call water when a guy walked through the flames and put them all out," I say, thinking of the jackass. I'm going to get him back for pointing me the wrong way to the headmasters' office and for being a general ass.

"This is your classroom, Miss Crowe," Mr. Daniels says, and I turn back to look at him.

"Thank you," I reply.

He runs a hand through his hair. "I'll see you Sunday in the gym at six and not a minute later," he instructs with a deadly serious face.

"In the afternoon?" I ask, concerned that he is going to say the morning. He only laughs.

"The morning, Mackenzie," he says my name softer than the rest of his words, and he turns to walk away. My eyes drop to the amazing ass he has in his tight clothes, then up to the muscular chest and soft-brown hair.

Damn. This teacher is going to be the death of me.

Chapter 7

KENZIE

"*Y*ou are ten minutes late, Miss Crowe," The old-looking teacher says. He stands as I walk through the door of the room. Looking up, I notice that the ceiling of the dome-shaped room is completely open, the open sky is allowing the sun to be our light in here. I spot Kelly sitting alone at the back of the room, with an empty seat next to her, smiling at me.

"I'm sorry. I was with the headmasters," I say, and the teacher nods. He must be in his sixties, with long, grey hair and a stern face covered in wrinkles.

"Please take a seat, and we will begin," he replies. It feels like every pair of eyes in the room is watching me as I walk toward the back of the room and take the seat next to Kelly.

"Hey, fire starter, I'm glad to see you're alright. I was getting worried. Have you done anything else I should know about?" Kelly whispers, and I smile at her.

"Does ogling the hot Mr. Daniels count?" I whisper, and she chuckles a little.

"Who is Mr. Daniels?" she asks. I go to whisper back, when I hear my name being called.

"Miss Crowe and Miss Curwood, you are first on my list. Please come to the middle of the room," the teacher says.

I stand up with Kelly, and we walk back toward the teacher. He smiles and gestures for us to stand in front of him.

"Now, class, I'm Mr. Lindeman, and my specialty is Divination. Divination is one the hardest powers to master and nearly impossible for most. The strongest of our people can only see a year or a little more into the future, so please bear this in mind. The future is never completely certain, nor is it completely clear in vision form," he explains. We all know this, but I'm hoping I can see a little of the future.

"Now, I want you to use your divination powers on each other. One at a time. Miss Crowe, why don't you go first?" he asks gently.

"Sure," I nod.

"Now, stand a foot away from each other and hold hands. Holding a connection to someone enables them to see whatever you see in the vision. When you are first learning to use your powers, recollection of the vision can be difficult. You will be partnered so if you are unable to remember what you saw, your partner should be able to fill you in," he explains. I nod and hold both my hands out, Kelly slides her hands into mine and winks at me.

"Please call on your mark, Miss Crowe," he says. I reach into my mind, calling on my mark and envisioning it in my head. The divination mark is a basic eye design, but the pupil of the eye is full of swirls. I picture the swirls moving, a constant motion, frequently changing direction. The minute I call it and close my eyes, the vision takes over.

"Kelly, the amount of powers you have means nothing to me. I've always just wanted you," a male voice says as I open my eyes. I can't see anything, and I recognise the voice, but I can't place it. The room is black, and as I watch, two blurry figures come into view.

"I-I can't do this. I'm sorry, but you're with them, and they have her!" Kelly shouts. I feel a tugging sensation that causes me to close my eyes and when I open them, I'm back at the academy.

"What did you see?" The teacher asks, but Kelly softly shakes her head. She doesn't need to say anymore.

"Myself, eating a big, bacon sandwich tomorrow morning," I say, and he nods, like he expected that. I don't know who Kelly was speaking to, but I have the feeling she does by the way she is blushing and looking away from me. *Who could it have been?*

"Very good job, now it's your turn Miss Curwood," the teacher says, gesturing at her to begin.

I watch as Kelly closes her eyes, and my eyes widen as she starts faintly glowing white. Actually glowing. I don't get to look for long before I feel a pulling sensation, and I close my eyes.

"Kenzie!" a man roars, his voice filled with both anger and worry. I open my eyes; to see fire everywhere and we are in the middle of the academy hall. I can see myself, standing holding my stomach in the middle of all the fire. My hair is covering my face as I look down at the floor, so I can't see my expression. I turn slightly to see a man running towards me, putting out the flames as he goes with water from his hands. It's the guy from earlier, the one that walked through the flames to put out the fire. He falls to his knees in front of me, just as I collapse into his arms.

"Enzo," I hear myself say, my voice sounds strange to me, but you can't miss the emotion in my voice. Why would I have any other emotion than hate for that jerk?

"Not like this, you are not leaving me, Crowe!" Enzo shouts, moving my hands and covering the wound with his own. Just as I watch myself pass out in his arms, I see him healing me and he moves his hands away, lifting my shirt a little to show the closed-up scar. Was I stabbed? Enzo picks me up, holding me close and places a kiss on my forehead. Why is the incredibly hot jerk kissing me?

"Is she?" Locke asks as he runs over, putting out more of the fire as he stops near Enzo, and Enzo shakes his head.

"No, but that fucking teacher who did this is going to pay for hurting her. I'm going to fucking kill him," Enzo spits out, the fury in his tone is the last thing I hear before I'm forced to close my eyes by the pull.

When I open my eyes again, I see Kelly's pure light-blue eyes open in shock, her whole body is still glowing white. The light suddenly disappears, and she collapses to the floor in a heap.

"Kelly!" I shout, going to catch her, but I miss. A wave of air stops her body from hitting the ground, holding her in the air. I look over to see Mr. Lindeman holding a hand out towards Kelly, air flowing from his hand. He gently lowers her onto the floor, and I fall to my knees, gently shaking her shoulder. I can hear the classroom whispering, but no one is brave enough to say anything out loud.

"She will be fine, class. The divination power is strong for her, and this sometimes happens. However, I have never seen a glow before," Mr. Lindeman says, his tone echoing the shock of his words as he comes to kneel next to her. He places his hands on her head, and I watch as he heals her, then moves his hands away. Kelly slowly blinks open her eyes, and stares at me, a vacant look in her eyes, her expression violently bare of any emotion.

"The portal will open," she says blankly, her eyes roll back, and then she passes out again.

What portal will open?

Chapter 8

KENZIE

*C*lutching onto Kelly's hand, I look down at her pale, unconscious face, my eyebrows drawing together in concern. I glance around the crappy excuse for a first aid room, mad that Kelly is currently lying across a few chairs, rather than on a bed. They're remodelling the actual first aid centre. *Fucking typical.*

Kelly stirs, and I instantly lean forward and stroke the hair from her face. "Kells? Sweetie, are you okay?" I whisper softly.

"Kennie?" she mumbles. *Oh Gods.* She hadn't called me Kennie since we were eight years old.

"It's Kenzie," I mutter.

"Kennie-kenz," she mumbles back, a smile taking over her face as her blue eyes flutter open. Seeing the expression take back over her face fills me with relief. *She's okay.* Despite the healer's reassurances, I wasn't accepting the fact my best friend was okay until I saw it for myself. I sit back in my seat, allowing myself to get a little more comfortable as Kelly slowly moves into a sitting position.

"Do you remember what happened?" I ask softly, still holding onto her hand and rubbing it soothingly.

"Um, the last thing I remember was you lying about your vision and saying it was about eating a bacon sandwich, which kind of made me feel hungry . . .," she trails off as a mortified look takes over her face. "Oh Gods, I did it wrong, didn't I? I didn't have a vison and instead knocked myself out like an idiot in front of the whole class," she whispers in a horrified tone.

"No, Kells, complete opposite. You had a killer vision, and you glowed. You freaking glowed! The teacher was going on about how powerful your divination skill must be the whole way down to the first aid room!"

"I glowed?" she asks, awe in her voice.

"You did," I answer, smiling brightly at her. Happy that although she only has two gifts, one of them is already proving to be so strong.

"Not many seers glow, Kenzie," she says, bobbing up and down in excitement. She is right about that. I only know of one other Marked that can glow, and she has a seat on one of the councils. Kelly's parents are going to be so proud of her.

"I know, it's so damn cool!"

"How long have I been in here?" she questions, suddenly looking a little more concerned as she takes in the sorry excuse for a first aid room.

"Um," I glance at the clock on the wall, as tradition it's symbolized with the twelve marks, rather than numbers. "About forty minutes," I answer.

"Why didn't they use a healer to wake me?" she asks sceptically.

"Mr. Lindeman tried to, but you woke for a second and then went back out. The healers decided to allow you to wake naturally after that. They suspected the vision exhausted you, so they were letting you rest," I answer softly.

"That's kind of scary," she whispers. "We were holding hands during the vision, what did I see?" I go to answer her, and explain the whole story, when a feeling in my gut strikes me.

"Nothing much really. It was me, and some other people. I think maybe in a class or something. I think that it was the fact the vision was so clear and intense feeling that it wiped you out," I lie smoothly, shooting her a smile. She frowns for a moment, before shrugging and leaning back in her seat.

"I guess that could be it," she says.

"Must be," I reply. *There's no need to stress her out about what she saw in that vision. She's already stressing enough. I can figure out whatever it means on my own.*

"You did wake up for a second and said "the portal will open", do you remember what portal?" I ask her, knowing she might hear from the other students about what she said as they all heard.

"Portal?"

"Yep," I nod.

"I remember seeing fire and something blue," she says, going a little pale again.

"It doesn't matter. Let's just leave it for now, okay?" I ask, and she nods.

"Am I allowed to leave?" she asks.

"Yup, healer said as soon as you felt okay to, we could go. She did take a look over you while you were unconscious, and she couldn't find anything wrong. Just told me to make sure you take it easy," I answer.

"Okay, can we go back to our room? Or do we have to go back to class?" she asks, her voice a little wobbly.

"Room, definitely." Standing up, I reach across and offer a hand to help her up, which she takes. Once on our feet, we make our way out of the makeshift, first aid room. I sign Kelly out on the clipboard by the door, so they don't worry where we've gone. We weave through the quiet halls; the majority of students are currently still in lessons.

As we step out into the courtyard, I hear someone shouting. I look around, but I can't spot the source of the noise.

"Up here, Kenzie!" the voice yells. *Up?*

I turn my head up and catch sight of Easton hanging out of a window. A third-floor window. And, he's about to fucking jump.

"EAST!" I scream as he jumps. At first, he falls quickly, then suddenly his descent slows, so he's floating down softly. *Air. East has an air mark. Breathe, Kenzie, breathe.*

He lands on the floor gracefully, and smirks, the

amusement reaching his eyes. "Worried, were you?" he teases, as he walks over to us.

"You may have given me a slight heart attack," I admit begrudgingly.

"You totally freaked, were you worried about his pretty face being ruined?" Kelly points out, laughing at the mortified expression on my face. *Drop me in it, why don't you Kells*.

"No!" I snap.

"You don't think I have a pretty face?" East asks, stepping closer to me. "I'm hurt, offended, and not at all amused, Mackenzie," he says softly, danger lacing his teasing tone.

"I-I never said that," I stammer out. *Great. Now, that was so smooth*.

"So, you do think I'm good looking?" he asks, smiling even wider. *Smug ass*.

"No, I just meant that your face is probably considered pretty, hell maybe even a touch feminine, actually. You're not really my type," I say, keeping my face as blank as possible.

"What? You can't be serious? Feminine?" he sputters, running a hand through his stupidly perfect hair.

"What? Shocked the whole world doesn't want to bang you?" I ask, smiling.

"Well, not the whole world, but I'm pretty sure the female population of the school does. And, 'feminine' is not the word to describe me, definitely not," he says confidently.

"Well, not me," I answer. "Why don't you go find

one of those other members of the female population to fall at your feet, East. You may do better with them," I retort.

"Well, I could do that. But, I prefer a challenge." He winks at me and steps back. "I'll catch you later then, Kenzie!" he says, turning to leave.

"Wait, what did you want?"

"Oh, shit, I meant to ask about what happened in your fire lesson," he says, turning back to us. "It's already been going around the whole school. Someone said you tried to fling a fireball at the teacher, is that true?"

"Of course, it's not true," Kelly interrupts with a laugh.

"Yeah, why would I throw a fireball at bitchface?" I ask, not really expecting an answer. "Then again, maybe I should have," I add, muttering under my breath.

"Then why is half of her hair missing?" Easton asks.

"Um, I kind of lost control and made fire tornadoes, oops?"

"'Oops'?" he mimics. "'Fire tornadoes'? Why am I not surprised?" Easton chuckles. "Pro-tip, don't mix fire and air unless you want to cause disaster," he says teasingly.

"Yeah, so I've since been told," I mumble. *Why did everyone else think of that but me?*

"Anyway, I need to get moving, just wanted to make sure you were okay, and that you weren't attacking teachers with fireballs."

"Well, I'm fine. Catch you later, East," I call after him as he walks off.

The second he's out of earshot, Kelly turns to me. "That man is sex on legs, and you know it," she says.

"Oh, I so do. You know who else is sex on legs," I say, wriggling my eyebrows.

"Oh Gods, Kenzie, you cannot go after Mr. Sexy, no matter how sexy he is," she replies, and starts moving towards our dorm building.

"Why not," I whine.

"Because Mr. Sexy is a teacher, and although not illegal for our kind because we don't even start school till we're seventeen, you know it's frowned upon. Your dads would freak for one, and he would be fired," she answers.

"I know, I know. But, he's so hot. Like, 'fuck me on your desk' hot," I reply.

"That hot, huh?" she asks, pulling a face.

"Yup. I'm not seriously going after the guy or anything, but I will say this, if you want to be with someone, you should be with them," I say, my tone losing its playfulness.

"You really think so?" she asks, looking thoughtful.

"Definitely," I answer without hesitation. "You can't help who you fall for."

"I think so, too," Kelly replies, linking her arm in mine.

"Come on, I have snacks under the bed, and I know you missed lunch."

"You're a Goddess," I reply, linking my arm back in hers as we make our way to our dorm room.

Chapter 9

KENZIE

"*N*ow class, because spirit is such a rare gift among our kind, we only have one class for all three year groups," the teacher explains as she comes to stand in front of her desk, her long skirt swishing around her ankles.

I shift in my seat and eye the five others in the small class room. No kidding, teach. We're all sitting in a small semi-circle, and sitting right next to me is none other than the asshole one minute, and kissing me in the vision of the future the next, Enzo. *Great.*

"Now we only have one new student blessed with Spirit this year, Mackenzie, welcome," she says warmly. I look up into her warm, welcoming face and relax a little. *Maybe this class won't be so bad.*

"Thank you, Miss . . .," I trail off, not knowing her name.

"Miss Dommett," she supplies for me. "But, call me Stacey, I hate formalities."

"Thank you, Miss Do—Stacey," I correct myself as I reply.

"Fabulous, let's make sure to make Mackenzie feel nice and welcome, guys," she says to the class. I notice for the first time that I'm the only girl in the class, which makes sense considering the male to female ratio of our kind. "For her benefit, let's go around and introduce ourselves."

"I'm Jack," the guy on the far right says, throwing a hand up in a mini-wave gesture.

"I'm Steve," the next in the line says.

"Ryan," the next says.

"Same name as my brother," I reply with a smile.

"Ryan Crowe?" he asks with a smile.

"That's the one," I reply.

"You really don't look like Ryan's sister, other than the black hair, maybe," he says.

"Everyone says that," I reply, returning his smile. Stacey turns to Enzo next and waits for a moment silently before a frown takes over her face.

"Lorenzo, aren't you going to introduce yourself?" Stacey asks, her tone losing its cheeriness.

"No, fire-starter, here, and I met yesterday," he says, throwing me a disgruntled look.

"And, here I was thinking we wouldn't have any classes together," I reply sarcastically. One could have hoped, anyway. I add silently.

"No such luck," he mutters under his breath, but I catch it.

"What is your problem?" I ask through gritted teeth, as Stacey turns back towards Jack to answer a question.

"You are my problem," he answers. "Thinking you're all that with your twelve marks."

I laugh. Not even attempting to keep the giggles in. *Like seriously, the guy is jealous about my twelve marks? I don't even want them!*

"What is funny, Mackenzie?" Stacey asks. That snaps me from my laughter. *Oops.*

"Nothing Mi—Stacey," I answer.

"It sure sounds like something was," she says, narrowing her eyes and glancing between me and Enzo.

"Just something Enzo said," I answer. *That's kind of the truth, anyway.*

"Yes, my little brother does have quite the sense of humour," she says, rolling her eyes.

Her little brother? You have got to be kidding me.

"Little brother, huh?" I direct my question to Enzo, whispering.

"She's the only spirit teacher in the school, there was no choice but to put me in her class when I was marked by spirit," he answers, shrugging.

"Now. I want everyone to tell me one thing they know about the spirit mark," Stacey asks and looks at Enzo with an arched eyebrow.

"The spirit mark makes it possible for us to see spirits that stay around for a short period of time after their deaths," Enzo answers in a bored tone.

"Mackenzie?" Stacey asks, and I try to think of

anything my dads and mum told me. My mum has spirit, but she always said it's useless. When she lost someone close to her, she couldn't see their spirit and since then, she never tries to use the power.

"That spirit is extremely unreliable," I answer, and she nods.

"Spirit is useful to find out clues for murders," Steve adds next.

"Ow," I say, when I feel something poke into my side. I turn to see Enzo smiling at me, holding a pencil in his hand which he is flicking between his fingers. I go to ignore him and listen to Stacey, when he does it again. I turn in time to see him use air to float his pencil back over to his hand.

"Stop poking me," I say through gritted teeth and he just shrugs, looking forward.

"Is there a problem, Mackenzie?" Stacey asks.

"No, Crowe was just flirting with me and graciously, I very gently let her down," Enzo answers, and I narrow my eyes at him as my cheeks start feeling warm.

"Well, if we could have your full attention, Mackenzie, that would be appreciated," Stacey says. Although, she shoots her brother a look that says just how much she buys what he said. He shrugs at her, not the least bit bothered. I nod and lean back in my chair, listening to the conversation she is having with Ryan about how we can see the spirits of animals as well as people when I feel a poke in my side.

I don't say anything this time, but I do glare at

him. He only looks back at me, his eyes drifting over my body slowly and then looking back at Stacey.

I don't think he is going to get a chance to save me in the future. No, there's more of a chance I'm going to try and kill him.

"How was spirit? See any ghosts?" Kelly asks as I sit next to her on the table at lunch. My eyes meet Enzo's, as he sits down next to a couple of guys at another table, and he smirks at me. *Jerk.*

"No, but I do have a guy in mind to kill and test if I can see his ghost," I say, and she laughs.

"Who?"

"The hot jerk who saved me from the fire. He just spent three hours poking me with a pencil," I say, nodding behind her. She turns to look at Enzo, and then she laughs loudly as she looks at me.

"Maybe he wants to *poke* you?" she says, and I glare at her as I pull my hair up into a high ponytail.

"He won't be doing any friggin *poking*, no matter how hot he is. He is still a jerk," I reply, and she laughs.

"Sure." She smiles, the humour in her voice is thick. *She doesn't believe me.*

A large hand slides down my arm as I look up to see Locke as he sits next to me. Locke looks amazing today, dressed in a tight, white shirt and brown shorts. My eyes drift to all the muscles under his shirt that I can see outlined.

"Hey, Kenz, how is my firestarter?" he asks, and I narrow my eyes at him as I pick up my sandwich.

"It was an accident," I reply, choosing to ignore his question, and he laughs. I freeze as he puts one of his big arms around my shoulders and whispers in my ear. His lips are so close, that they brush the top of my ear, and I can feel his warm breath on my neck.

"Guess what?" he says, and I struggle to swallow the bite of sandwich I have. Man, this guy smells nice up close, and the brief brush of his lips against my ear has given me goosebumps.

"What?" I ask, as my eyes look around the room and catch Enzo's. Enzo watches me and Locke, his eyes seeming darker than ever, and he gets up, storming out of the room in anger. *What is his problem?*

"We have water class together next. I personally can't wait to see you in a bikini," he says and brushes his lips against my ear one more time before moving away. He starts eating like he said nothing, and Kelly gives me a cheeky look. I did manage to find my phone last night in one of my suitcases I hadn't unpacked yet. The academy app is really cool and has my timetable, and a lot of other useful stuff on it. The water class had a note saying to wear a swimsuit, and then I was lost for an hour when I found the games.

"I have to go, but I'm sure Locke will take you to your next class," Kelly says as she stands up.

"Of course I will," Locke replies, and she winks at me before walking away. We eat the rest of our food in silence, with me being aware of how close Locke is to me the whole time.

"Come on, or we will be late," he says standing up and holding a hand out for me. I slide my hand into his. He doesn't let go as we walk out, instead he links our fingers together.

"The swimming pool is in the basement," Locke says as he walks to the doors of some elevators I didn't see before. They are under the stairs, hidden out of sight. Locke presses the button just as I hear the first bell ring. We get into the elevator, which only has one large green button. After pressing it, I feel my stomach jerk as it quickly descends. We reach the ground, and the elevator chimes.

Stepping out, we walk into a massive room. There's a huge, circular swimming pool in the centre of the room filled with sparkling, clear-blue water. The room has high ceilings and no windows, just bright lights on the walls. It's not dark at all in here with the pool floor lights too. On one side, is a row of twenty singular, changing rooms and waiting for us is a woman with long, grey hair. She smiles and walks over. The woman is wearing a black swimming costume, and despite her age she looks good in it. *I hope I look that good in a swimming costume at her age.*

"Please get changed and then meet us out here," she says. I nod, letting go of Locke's warm hand when we get to the empty changing rooms. I strip down inside, leaving on my red bikini and go to check my phone. It's flat. I know I should have left it on charge longer last night. *Damn academy game apps I stayed up playing.*

"Wow," I hear when I walk out of the changing

rooms, and Locke is standing a foot away from me. *I should be the one saying 'wow'.* Locke has on tight, blue shorts that show off way too much, and I can't look away. His chest is firm, with a clear eight-pack, and I can see quite a few marks all over him. When I finally look up to his bright eyes, he is staring at me, and he takes a little step forward.

"Class, come over," the teacher shouts, breaking apart whatever moment is happening between us. I walk over with Locke to the other eight people in the room with us. *This is a small class.*

"I'm Miss Betson, and welcome to intermediate water class," she says. *I wonder if I'm in the wrong class — shouldn't I be in the beginner's class?*

"So, I would like us all to pair up and get into the pool. We will start with a very simple test. I want you to swim to the bottom of the pool and sit down. The longer you can stay underwater will tell me all I need to know. Pairs go down together and remember to call your water mark," she says, and I nod.

"You're with me, Kenz," Locke says, his hand once again sliding into mine. I don't know why I don't pull away. *It's likely something to do with those abs I can't stop looking at.* We walk down the steps into the warm water and swim out to the deeper side.

"Ladies first," Locke says with a smirk, and I laugh. I call my water mark by imagining the shell-shaped mark, before lowering myself into the water. I swim down and open my eyes. It stings at first, but I force myself to ignore it. I cross my legs and sink the final part to the bottom of the pool. I resist the urge to smile when Locke sits in front of me, he smiles though and bubbles leave his mouth. It's not long before I know I have to swim up for air, and Locke follows me. I take a deep breath and wipe the water from my eyes.

"Brilliant timing. You were under five minutes, and for your first time that is impressive. Now, everyone please sit on the edge of the pool. Mr. Valentine and Miss Crowe, please come here," she asks, and I swim over.

"Mr. Valentine, I want you to make a water fountain, and, Miss Crowe, I want you to copy," she directs, and I watch as she swims away.

"Come closer, Kenz," Locke says, and I swim right in front of him. He pulls me tightly against his chest and every part of me seems to stick to him as I place my hands on his shoulders. I watch as he spreads both his hands out, the water instantly rises around us and shoots up into the air and falls around us like a fountain. I don't watch the water, only Locke as he smiles down at me and then winks as he moves his head closer to mine. I let go of his shoulders and float back a little. The water falls to the pool as he moves his hands away. *Jesus, I was so friggin close to kissing one of the sexy twins.*

"Well done, it is now your turn, Miss Crowe," the teacher shouts. I copy what Locke did, by holding my hands out.

"Just imagine the water going up," he suggests, and I nod. I call my water mark in my mind, thinking of the water going up. Nothing happens. I feel like my power is doing something and my hands are glowing blue when I look at them, but there is no water going up above us.

"Stop!" I hear the teacher shout, and I give Locke a quizzical look, but he is looking down. I follow his eyes to see the empty pool below us, and I realise what I've done.

I've lifted all the water in the pool into the air. And us, floating with it.

"Hold on to me and let go of the water, okay?" Locke says as he moves closer and wraps his arm around me. I hook my legs around his waist, and he nods at me after a second. I drop my hands, and the water falls with us as I wrap my arms around Locke's neck and hold in a scream as we fall. The sound of the water slapping against the pool fills my ears as I keep my eyes closed shut.

"Open your eyes, Kenz," Locke whispers close to my ear. I open my eyes to see us still in the air, hovering above the pool. Most of the water is outside the pool, and the teacher is standing with the other students by the changing rooms.

"We are flying," I say in awe.

"No, I am, and you're having a ride," he chuckles. I hold on tight as he moves us, and then slide off him when he lands by the edge of the pool. I hear clapping, and I watch as Miss Betson walks over to us as she claps her hands.

"Very impressive, Miss Crowe. I see Mr. Daniels was right to add Locke to this class to watch you," she says.

"Mr. Daniels made you watch me?" I ask him curiously.

"Yes, he asked us to his office this morning. Logan, Enzo, Easton, Stella, and I are going to be in all your classes until you have some control over your powers. We are the best at most of them. Mr. Daniels is watching you in the rest, except divination. He thinks you're safe in that one." Locke laughs.

"I'm not a child, and I don't need watching," I snap, placing my hands on my hips and glaring at him indignantly.

"They are just there to help you, Miss Crowe. You have a lot of power, and if Locke hadn't helped you today, you could have seriously hurt yourself," Miss Betson says, sounding reasonable, and it annoys me.

"Fine," I mutter, and Locke winks at me. Miss Betson walks over to the other students, and Locke steps closer to me.

"You may not like having us all watching you, but I know you liked me getting close to you in that pool. I won't forget that," he whispers and walks away. I can't take my eyes off him as he crosses the room to the changing area, the way the water drips down his muscles, the confidence in his walk.

He isn't wrong, damn him.

Chapter 10
KENZIE

I frown at the paper on the floor as I walk back into the bedroom from the adjoining bathroom. Kelly is a neat freak, so I doubt she left it there. I cross my room and pick the paper up. The letters M C are written across the front. Turning it over, I frown as I read the strange message printed on the back.

Mackenzie Crowe,
If you want to live to see your life outside of the Marked
Academy, meet me in the abandoned dorm building by the
forest at Midnight.
Come alone, and don't be caught by the monitors on duty.
There will be consequences if you fail to comply.
—A

What the actual fuck? I re-read the message again

and again, trying to discern what the hell this could be about, when I notice the symbol drawn at the top of the note. The twelfth mark. *Shit. This can't be good.*

I stuff the note into my back pocket and pull my jacket on. I'd slept in and missed breakfast, having told Kelly to go on without me earlier. My bed was just way too comfy this morning. Or rather, I was just way too tired. I didn't get much sleep, constantly replaying Kelly's vision in my head trying to figure out what it could possibly mean. I just know it's something important, something I need to figure out.

Making my way from the dorm to my first and only class of the day, I'm relieved there is just the one on Saturday. Although, I'm nervous about this class more than any other.

How can a technophobe be expected to perform technomancy?

I follow the directions on my map app, surprised when it leads me away from the main building and towards the forest. I frown at the old, unused dorm building as I pass it, not able to shake the sketchy feelings it gives me. I continue walking along the edge of the forest until it thins out, revealing a lush, green field filled with flowers. A woman whom I assume to be the teacher is sitting crossed-legged on the ground, looking like she is meditating. *Did I stumble into an earth class by mistake?* A few other students who I recognise, but haven't spoken to, are hovering around looking as unsure as I am.

"Sit down, class," she calls softly, not opening her eyes, or moving from her meditation position. We all sit awkwardly around her in a lose semi-circle. Someone sits closely behind me, I turn around and catch Enzo's dark eyes staring daggers at me.

"What's your problem?" I mutter.

"You. Thanks to you, I now have an extra class on Saturday, just because they don't trust you without a babysitter. I already passed all three years' worth of exams for this stupid class, and now I'm stuck taking it from the beginning again," he replies bitterly.

"Wait, how did you manage to complete all three years' worth already?" I ask.

"I've already completed three of my classes, I'm in an advanced class for another five," he snaps. "What, surprised I'm not just good looking?"

"You're good looking?" I ask, forcing a surprised, questioning tone into my voice. He scowls and gestures his hand forward.

"Just turn around and pay attention," he snaps.

"Sure, whatever. I'm just going to pretend that you're not here," I answer sweetly.

"And, I'll pretend that I'm anywhere but here," I hear him comment as I turn back around to face the teacher. The teacher must be in her late thirties, but she isn't dressed like it at all. A mixture of punk rock chick and hippy vibes shining through from her choice of attire. Her bright, bubble-gum pink-coloured hair is in bunches, with several beads and other accessories woven in with bright fabrics. A pair of aviator sunglasses sit atop her head, and thick, beaded bracelets cover up both of her arms.

She opens her eyes, and I'm surprised by the

mismatched pair that stare right at me knowingly, as if she could feel my inspection. One eye is a shade of murky brown, and the other a sky blue.

"Welcome class to your first lesson of Technomancy, my name is Miss Arthur," she says softly, her voice tranquil. Although she's speaking to the whole class, I feel as if she is talking directly to me. "Now, I know a few of you must be feeling confused, bewildered even. How will we learn the basics of technomancy without any technology? These are questions every beginner student has, technomancy has a lot of misconceptions. That those adept at technomancy are all computer geeks is probably the main one. However, I am one of the most proficient in my gift within this country." She pauses, and I glance around noticing everyone is entranced by her. Other than Enzo, who is smiling slightly while looking up at the sky. "I am one of the most computer challenged people you will ever meet, I can't even connect my phone to human run WI-FI. Thank the gods that ours connects to all marked devices automatically," she finishes and smiles at the class, a dazzling white smile. A girl with dark hair, streaked with lighter brown raises her hand from in the front.

"Yes, Miss Wilson?" Miss Arthur asks.

"Then what is technomancy if it's not all computers? Isn't technomancy magic in tech?" she asks in a somewhat belligerent voice.

"Technomancy is the use of magic in technology, that is correct. What you have incorrect is how you define technology," she replies, not the least bit perturbed by the girl's attitude. "Can anyone here define technology for me?" We all sit silently, nobody wanting to look like an idiot in the first lesson.

"Fine. Enzo, would you be so kind as to define technology for me?" she asks, shooting him a warm smile that crinkles the corners of her eyes.

"Technology is a means to fulfil a purpose," he answers, as if repeating something he's heard a thousand times. "Technomancy is the use of magic, in that mean, to fulfil a purpose," he adds, in the same reciting tone.

"Excellent, thank you, Enzo. Do you have any questions, class?"

Tons. I glance around and see nobody else putting their hand up. *Nope, not drawing any more attention to myself.*

"Well then, let us begin. First, a brief history of technology, and how technomancy has linked with technology through the years." I hear Enzo snort behind me. I shuffle back and to the side to sit beside him.

"What's so funny?" I whisper, as Miss Arthur starts talking about early human, technological advances.

"Brief history," he says quietly with a smirk. I pull a confused face and he sighs. "She'll go on about the wonders of technology and technomancy in history for most of your lessons."

"Oh," I say softly. *Fuck, I always hated history in school.*

"It takes her a long time to get to the good stuff," he says in a hushed tone.

"What's the good stuff?" I ask, shooting a worried glance to the teacher to make sure she hasn't noticed us chatting.

"How you put the magic into the mean," he answers. "It's like skipping a step. You take the basic, human-created tool, fuel it with magic for the means, and boom, technomancy."

"I don't get it," I mutter, frowning.

"Okay, say you have a human designed phone, but it has no signal where you are because of human technology limitations. You'd use technomancy to boost the signal," he explains softly.

"Why doesn't she just say that?" I mutter back.

"Because she likes the sound of her own voice, I think she should have gone into acting personally," he replies with a grin.

I look back to Miss Arthur, who is still blabbing about the same thing as she was before. *I think he might be right. Damn.*

"When do we start using magic in this class?" I ask.

"About halfway," he says.

"That's not so bad," I reply.

"Halfway through the year, that is."

"You have got to be kidding me," I say. Seeing the serious, commiserative expression on his face says it all.

Looks like I won't be dealing with my technophobia anytime soon then.

Chapter 11

KENZIE

J zip up my black hoodie and mentally kick myself for not wearing more layers. I walk within the tree line, using the cover to shield me from the sight of the main buildings. The last thing I want to do is get caught out after curfew. *Curfew, it's ridiculous; I'm seventeen, not seven. Like any self-respecting teenager is going to stay inside their dorm.* I roll my eyes at the thought and then focus back on the task at hand, getting to the dorm without getting caught.

I spot the old dorm building in the distance as I approach. Casting my eyes across every inch of the building, I look for any sign of activity or life, but there is nothing. *This can't be good. Shit, why am I doing this?*

I make my way around to the back of the building, wanting to scout out the place before I sneak in, somehow. *Gods, how am I even meant to get into a locked building? Cat burglar I am not.*

The fire exit door at the back provides the answer for me, as it's been left ajar, presumably by whomever sent me the note. *Shit, if I go in that way they'll see me coming for sure.*

I look more closely at the building. *Bingo.* I notice a window on the 1st floor isn't shut all the way. I walk closer and try to work out how to get to the window. I stand there, feeling clueless for a while when it hits me. East jumping from the window. I could use my air ability to get up there. I'd already managed to call on it once during the fire lesson. *How hard could it be?*

I picture the air mark in my head and try to call on it. I picture the air lifting me. I look down, feet firmly still planted on the ground. *Damn it!*

"Why are you staring at a wall, Crowe?" Enzo's voice drifts over to me. I turn to see him walking over from the shadows of the trees. Enzo looks every bit the bad boy he comes across as. With his leather coat, heavy, black boots, and denim jeans. His black hair is styled to the side, and even in the dim light I can see how dark his eyes are as he watches me. *Why are bad guys so friggin sexy?*

"Did you invite me here?" I ask, and he chuckles.

"Not even in your dreams," he says slowly, and I have the feeling he is checking me out as he walks past. I don't reply to his remark as he walks around me, but I do glare at him. I watch as he walks into the building through the fire exit. *Fuck it.* I follow him in, feeling the cold wash of a ward hitting me, just before the blasting music hits my ears. It's not too loud, but I'm guessing the ward is a sound blocker. The abandoned building has a massive party going on inside. There are three huge speakers at the front of the room and a table full of alcohol at the side. There are chairs littered around and people dancing to the music. The girls look half dressed in skimpy dresses, and I look down at my jeans and hoodie. *I clearly didn't get the memo. There must be about hundred people in here* I think as I look around. I catch a glance of Enzo's back before he disappears into the crowd of people. I walk around for a bit, not seeing anyone I know and jump when Enzo stops next to me.

"You should leave," he says, and I look up at him.

"Why?" I ask, and he doesn't respond to me, but gives me a look that suggests I'm stupid or something. I watch as he walks away.

"Kenzie Crowe, right?" a woman's seductive voice says next to me. I turn a little to see that Stella girl standing next to me, her arms crossed and a sweet smile on her pretty face. *Shit, this girl is pretty, and it makes me want to hide in a corner*. She has curly, blonde hair, a stick-thin figure with big boobs, and the heels she has on make her taller than me. Her dark-red dress matches the red lipstick she has on. I want to think it looks slutty, but my mind betrays me by thinking how nice the outfit is with the lipstick.

"Yes, you're Stella, right?" I say, and she smiles widely.

"I see you've heard of me. Welcome to this year's

welcome party," she says holding out a hand. I don't take it as I think over her words.

"Why was my friend not invited?" I ask her. If this was a welcome party for first years, Kelly should be here.

"Who?" she asks, a slightly annoyed frown on her face as she pulls her hand back slowly.

"Kelly Curwood." I say, watching as she laughs.

"The two?" she chuckles out, and I narrow my eyes at her.

"Oh, hunny, we only let seven and ups in here. You should get some better friends, rather than that *weakling*. She might as well leave the academy now. She would be better with the humans, I mean, she basically is one. Such a waste of space," she says, and I don't think as I slap her. Her head swishes to the side, and she glares back at me as she straightens up. *That felt good.*

"You shouldn't have done that, you little bitch," she says, wiping the blood from her lip.

"I'm not the one who's a bitch," I say. I won't let her speak about Kelly like that. Stella doesn't reply, but she grabs my arm quickly. Pain slams into me and filters though every part of my body. Falling to my knees as I scream, the pain just keeps flowing through me. Wave after wave. I can't think straight. I try to pull my arm away, but her fake nails dig into my arm as she holds on tight.

"Let her go," Enzo's voice comes through all the pain, his words are clipped and full of anger. I take a deep breath the minute Stella's hand falls away from my arm. My knees give, and I begin to fall to the ground, but someone catches me. I feel a large arm slide under my knees as someone lifts me up.

"The stupid twelfth girl needed to be taught a lesson about her place," Stella says.

"You need to fuck off, Stella, this shit isn't cool. She has had her powers a week. Just one fucking week. Winning a fight against her is nothing to be proud of," Enzo replies. I faintly register that it's him holding me, but everything is still fuzzy. I burrow my head into his chest, smelling his leather jacket and a faint smell that reminds me of a bonfire.

"Whatever," Stella says flippantly, and I feel Enzo moving with me.

"Why did you help me?" I whisper when the music of the party disappears and chilly air hits my face. Enzo doesn't reply for what seems like a long time, but I know he heard me.

"I don't know, Crowe," he replies softly, and everything goes black.

"YOU HAVE GOTTA WAKE UP, CROWE," a deep voice flitters through to me as I pull my eyes open. Every part of my body aches, reminding me of last night. That Stella girl is a bitch. I resist the urge to move when I look up and see Enzo hovering over me, his face too close, and I see how dark his eyes are this close. They really do look nearly black, I find myself struggling to look away. *They are something else.* I blink when he straightens up, standing by the bed. I sit up and look around at the dimly lit room. *This is not my bedroom.*

"Enzo?" I ask, looking around the big room. There are two single beds in here, and there is a guy with light-blond hair lightly snoring in the other bed. There are two large wardrobes, and I notice straight away how much bigger their room is compared to mine and Kelly's. *That's so not fair.* I feel myself quickly, noticing I'm wearing the same clothes as the party last night. Enzo must have looked after me.

"You have gotta go before Logan wakes up," Enzo says quietly, nodding a head towards the blond man who stirs in his bed.

"Too late, dickhead. Kenzie, is that you?" Logan's sleepy voice drifts over to me as he rolls over. I watch as he grins at me as he sits up in bed, shirtless and looking amazing. His blond hair is messy and all over his face but it's not that I'm looking at. No, it's his muscular chest, the marks covering his heart and ribs. He has quite a few, just like his twin.

"Hey," I say, pulling myself out of the bed and stretching. My shoes and coat are missing, I notice as my feet touch the cold floor.

"What are you doing in Enzo's bed, and why wasn't I invited?" Logan asks with a wink that makes me blush.

"Crowe decided to pick a fight with Stella, and it didn't go well," Enzo answers dryly.

"Shit, your ex? That girl is fucking crazy," Logan

says, suddenly looking much more awake as his eyes widen.

"You dated her?" I ask Enzo, and he narrows his eyes on me.

"For a bit. It wasn't my best decision. She got a little crazy," he says.

"How?" I ask with a chuckle that makes him groan.

"She's stalking him and making sure no girl goes near him in this place. There are some rumours going around," Logan answers. I chuckle as Enzo uses his air mark to slam a book off the side table. It hits Logan in the chest.

"Ouch, dickhead. I didn't say they were true," he says.

"They aren't true," Enzo grits out and mutters something under his breath that I can't hear.

"Why the fuck are we all up on a Sunday, at five am?" Logan asks, and I look over to see him on his phone.

"Crowe has training with Mr. Daniels at six. She doesn't want to be late," Enzo replies. *Shit, how am I going to do class when I feel like this?*

"I feel like crap," I reply, and he nods.

"That's what happens when people use the pain mark on you. I healed you, but you won't feel good for a day or so. Stella's most powerful mark is pain, she could have killed you and might have after you hit her. Stella will only see you as competition. You need to learn how to ward yourself," Enzo says, his tone can't be mistaken for anything other than a warning. I shiver as I remember the pain I felt, it was like being stabbed in every part of my body. I couldn't focus enough to call any of my powers. I have a feeling I'm lucky Enzo was there and saved me. *Again.*

"She used what?" Logan asks, getting out of his bed and coming over to stand in front of me. I freeze as he brushes a stray hair away from my face. His finger skims over my cheek as I take a deep breath. Man, this guy is hot. *Why are there so many hot marked here?*

"I slapped her for speaking about Kelly like shit. What the hell was that party anyway?" I ask, my voice a little too high-pitched, and I inwardly groan. If Logan notices, he doesn't say anything, and he moves away a little. I notice that Enzo has left the room, leaving the door slightly open. I didn't even get to say thank you to the jerk.

"Stella throws a party every year, only for higher ups. It's a shit party, anyway. Kelly didn't miss out on much," he says.

"Still. I hate how she looked down on Kelly for having two powers."

"It's our world. Now come on, let's go get some breakfast, and I'll walk you to class as I'm already up," Logan says as he goes to his side of the room and gets some clothes out. I turn around when he just pulls his shorts off in front of me. Boy, this guy is confident and from what I caught a glance at, he should be. I spot my shoes by the door and slip them on. I find my coat on the back of the door and feel the pockets, finding my phone, but it's flat. Damn, Kelly must be worried.

"Let's go," Logan says, and his hand slides into mine as we walk down the quiet corridor. I don't question his hand in mine, not when I just saw what he looks like naked. *Gods, I can't stop thinking about his body.*

"What classes do we have together?" I ask, remembering he was one of the students Mr. Daniels asked to watch me.

"Earth class. I was going to be in your pain class, but it clashes with one of my electives. So, unfortunately, Stella volunteered for that one. Ask Mr. Daniels to teach you how to ward, it's easy, and I would show you if we had time," he says. *Great, more pain from the wannabe Barbie bitch.*

We don't say much more as we walk through the quiet corridors, it's strange to see it this empty, but I know it's because everyone is still in bed. Where I should be. Fucking detention every Sunday.

"Are the kitchens even open?" I ask, and he nods.

"Yeah, they have food out twenty four hours a day now. The transmutation students get really hungry after a shift and some of those classes are at night, depending on what you shift into," he explains as we go down the stairs. *I wonder what I will shift into?*

We both grab our food when we get to the dining hall. I choose cereal as there is no cooked food at this time of day, and he gets the same as me. We're munching on our cereal in companionable silence, when his phone goes off. He clicks it open and smiles at the phone, accepting a videocall.

"East man, what are you doing awake?" he asks.

"Kelly just came to find me, she can't find Kenzie, and I'm—" he stops when Logan cuts him off.

"Wait, no worries. She was in our bedroom last night, that's all," Logan explains.

"What?" East shouts down the phone. I hear Kelly's voice in the background, and I get up, walking around the table so I can see her.

"You could have texted me, Kenz. I've been worried," Kelly says once I can see her in the phone.

"Sorry. It's a long story, but I passed out. Enzo healed me and let me sleep in his bed," I say, instantly regretting giving my explanation now over the phone. *Shit, she looks even more worried.*

"You okay?" she asks.

"Yeah, I'll explain later. I've gotta go to detention. You know the one with Mr. Daniels," I say, and she wiggles her eyebrows.

"I'm sure he can make you feel better," she says, making me laugh.

"I doubt it, Mr. Daniels is a beast of a teacher. Everyone is scared of their classes with him, and no one has ever beaten him in a fight," Logan tells me.

"Shit, that's impressive. What is he doing being a teacher if he has skills like that? He could work for the council," I reply.

"I heard his sister is a rebel, and that's why he won't work for them. He won't hunt her." East says coming back into view of the camera with a worried look.

"Makes sense, I guess."

"Shit, we need to go. You're gonna be late," Logan

says and turns the phone off before I can say goodbye. I look up at the clock, seeing it's already ten minutes past six.

Great way to make an impression Kenz, turning up late to your first detention.

Chapter 12

KENZIE

I enter into the dark classroom and wonder where the heck the light switch is. It's almost pitch-black in here.

I feel across the wall blindly for the switch, when someone grabs me from behind and throws me. I prepare myself to hit hard ground, but instead hit a soft, cushiony feeling . . . *a mat?* A light flickers on, and Mr. Daniels is standing over me, holding a hand out.

"You need to work on your awareness, Miss Crowe. Had I been an actual attacker, you would be dead right now," he says softly, a satisfied-looking smile on his face. As if he finds that amusing. I'm seeing why Logan said that the other students are scared of him. He's every bit a dangerous animal. I notice he is wearing gym clothes: light-grey joggers and a clingy, white t-shirt. No shoes on, and no glasses either. His eyes look even more enticing without his glasses on. I take his hand nervously and allow him to pull me up. The second I'm on my feet, he blasts me back onto my ass with a gust of air magic.

"What the fuck!" I shout. "Why help me up just to knock me back down?" I question, feeling baffled at his logic.

"You're going to end up on your ass a lot today, Miss Crowe. In fact, for the rest of the year unless you improve," he answers. The look of disdain on his face says just how much he thinks that is likely to happen.

"Any reason you are knocking me on my ass? What kind of detention class is this?" I snap.

"There are several reasons we are knocking you on your ass, Miss Crowe," he says, offering out his hand again. I take it and stand, this time quickly moving as far across the room as possible to get away from him. He smiles somewhat devilishly at the sign of my quick retreat. "Better," he says quietly. A gust of air hits me from behind, pushing me to my hands and knees. *Fucking asshole.* "But, my magic can hit you even if you do try and hide on the other side of the room. You need to be prepared to block my magic, to attack back."

"I barely know how to use any of my powers yet, let alone know how to block someone else's! This isn't fair," I spit, standing up without his assistance this time.

"Life isn't fair, Miss Crowe," he replies, not seeming the least bit bothered by my anger at the situation. "My job is to teach you just that, and other things. You wanted to know why you will be falling on your ass every Sunday for the next year?" he asks.

"Yes," I admit begrudgingly.

"First, thanks to your twelve marks, you're a target. You need to know how to protect yourself. Second, because falling on your ass is the best way to learn. And, finally, because we are going to see if we can trigger your twelfth mark," he answers smoothly. I try and process his answers, feeling my heart beat faster at the mention of being a target, but something else sticks out more.

"Trigger my twelfth mark? But, we don't even know what it does," I question.

"Exactly. The headmasters have asked me to try and assist you in finding that out."

"And, knocking me on my ass is supposed to answer that question? Nobody knows what the bloody twelfth mark is!" I reply. "Me falling on my ass is so likely to change that, right?" I add sarcastically.

"Yes, it will. Because right now, Miss Crowe, tell me how fast your heart rate is? Tell me, are you feeling panicked, can you feel the adrenaline running through you?"

"Yes, but what does that have to do with the mark?" I ask, watching him slowly stalk closer toward me.

"Marks can be triggered accidentally. Normally, when the person in question is feeling a surge of adrenaline," he answers quietly. I go to respond, but he moves so quickly I barely register the attack. He's grabbed me and spun me around, holding me locked against him, my back to his front. "We need to get your pulse racing, Miss Crowe," he whispers in my ear. He pushes me harshly away from him, and I turn back around to face him feeling stunned. I notice that his white workout top is clinging tightly to his impressive body. I *can think of a few better ways he could get my pulse racing.*

The sound of a throat clearing makes me look back up at his face, he raises an eyebrow questioningly at me. *He wants me to attack, right? I can do that.* I plant an innocent look on my face, as I'm thinking of the air mark in my head. I call on it, hoping it's more responsive than it was last night. He gives me a curious look, and I feel the power answer me. Without hesitating, I direct it to knock into the back of his legs. He sidesteps my tiny gust with ease, like it would have knocked him anyway.

"Damn it," I curse.

"You'll have to do better than that," he says.

"Before you, you know, knock me on my ass again, can you please show me how to protect myself against pain magic?" I ask, remembering what Logan said earlier. He frowns at my question.

"You won't need that in your pain lessons for a few weeks at least, Miss Crowe, why would you like to specifically know that right now?"

"No reason," I answer too quickly.

"You do seem a little worn down," he says softly, approaching me slowly. He rests a hand against my forehead and closes his eyes, as if concentrating. I feel a slight wave of magic roll through me, a probing feeling.

"What are you doing?" I ask quietly, not wanting to put him off and have him accidentally fry my brain or something.

"I'm using my healing ability to sense for illness or injury in your body," he answers stoically, opening his eyes. "Now, Miss Crowe, I am only going to ask you once, so think very carefully before you try and refuse to answer me."

"Um . . . okay?" I mumble, stepping back slightly.

"Who the fuck used the pain mark on you? I know it couldn't have been in a class, you haven't had that lesson yet. Not that anyone in a class would be pumping that much juice into it," he says.

I think about it for a moment. There is no use denying it happened, but that doesn't mean I need to tell him anything. I can deal with bitches like Stella myself.

"I smacked someone, they used pain on me. I'm not telling you who, or why, it's none of your business," I respond, narrowing my eyes at him. Just daring him to try and push me on the matter. He takes me by surprise, when instead, he just nods his head slightly, as if accepting my answer.

"Did you have a good reason for hitting them?" he asks.

"Yes, I think I did," I answer.

"Well, considering their means of retaliation, I would believe it." He sighs and runs a hand through his sexy hair.

Damn it, Kenzie, stop checking your teacher out. I look away, trying not to stare at him any more than is appropriate to look.

"Look at me, Miss Crowe," he demands. I turn my head back towards him, and stare into his determined, green eyes. "You know what the protection mark looks like, yes?" he asks.

"Yes," I say, nodding. It would be hard not to, considering it's on my skin.

"Describe it to me, as you picture it," he says softly, taking my hand in his. I shiver from the touch.

"Um, it looks like a shield. A shield with an eye on it," I say, trying to picture the exact image in my head.

"Now imagine that shield in front of you, protecting you," he softly instructs.

"Okay." I close my eyes.

"Are you doing it now?" he asks.

"Yes," I answer. Suddenly I feel slight, tiny pinpricks stabbing into my hand. I gasp and try to pull my hand away from him, but he holds on tight.

"Sorry, but you have to feel a slight pain to defend against it. Imagine that shield, call on your mark." I do as he says, but still I can feel that same pinprick pain on my hand.

"It isn't working," I moan.

"Try to imagine the shield changing shape, imaging it growing, and surrounding you completely in a bubble. Tighten the bubble to your skin. Visualisation is key," he coaches me on. I do as he says.

"Still not working," I mutter.

"Call harder on your mark, the visualisation may

have taken your concentration away from the mark itself." I do as he says, and the pinprick pain stops. I open my eyes and smile at him.

"Got it," I say happily. He releases his hold of my hand, and I rub it with my other one, still feeling tingly.

"You're a quick learner," he remarks, making me smile. I go to reply, when suddenly a gust of wind knocks me on my ass again.

"You ass!" I snap, and then a mortified expression takes over my face. *Oops?* I wait for him to tell me off for back chatting, but he just laughs.

"You really need to work on your awareness," he says, and then laughs some more.

Yeah, laugh it up now, Mr. Daniels. I narrow my eyes on him. *I'm going to get you back one day, and it won't just be you landing on your perfect ass.*

Chapter 13

KENZIE

*L*ying on top of my bedcovers stretched out like a starfish, I barely flinch as Kelly loudly lets herself into the room, clumsily slamming the door behind her.

"Hey, Kenz," she greets cheerily.

I only groan in response. My whole body is aching. If I thought Mr. Daniels was going to take it easy on me after finding out that I had been zapped with pain, I was very wrong. We spent the next three hours with him effectively just knocking me to the ground a hundred or so times. He also was shooting jets of icy-cold water at me, which I was meant to dodge or block. My clothes were drenched, and my body was aching. I clearly did a sucky job at both of those things.

"That bad, huh? Yeah, East was saying that he was a slave driver," Kelly says with a laugh. *East? When was she with East?* I try to stamp down on the jealous feeling that rises in me. *He probably mentioned it when she was looking for me earlier. But, why did she go to East to find me?*

"East?" I mumble, trying to make it sound casual.

"Yup! Easton was talking for a good hour about how hardcore Mr. Daniels is, total man-crush I think. Logan and Locke were the same. They seem to worship him like a god," she chatters away, almost mindlessly. I try to ignore the pangs I feel at her mentioning each of them. *Do I like them, too? Ugh, play it cool, Kenzie.*

"Did they mention me at all today?" I ask, and then immediately cringe. *Cool as a fucking cucumber.*

"Oh. My. Gods!" Kelly says, her voice excited. *Oh no.* "You like them, don't you!" she accuses.

"They're attractive," I grumble, wishing my bed would just swallow me whole.

"You know I'm not into them right, Kenz? Even if I was, you'd have nothing to worry about," she replies.

"Of course, I would have something to worry about, you're a knockout, Kells," I say, and she narrows her eyes at me. I'm sure she is going to come back with some remark when my iPad starts buzzing. I groan as I roll on my side and grab it. I accept the Facetime call and two of my dads' faces come into view, way too close to the camera. They're so close I can just see two noses. Despite the fact they both have technomancy marks, they are useless with technology.

"Move back guys, you're too close," I say with a small laugh.

"Little Kennie! We miss you, baby," Dad P says

when they both move and hold their iPad a good distance away. I groan when I hear that nickname; they all call me it. Thank God that East doesn't, he heard it enough. Dad P has wavy, blond hair, bright-green eyes, and a cheeky smile as he leans back a little. I know it's likely he isn't my real dad, but he has been in every way that's possible.

"Hey Dad!" I say, and Dad L replies to me. Dad L has short, black hair and a serious expression. I would assume he is my biological dad, but who knows? My mum has dark hair too. Ryan has dark hair too, but he has bright-green eyes, so I always guessed he might be Dad P's son. I laugh when I see him being shoved out of the way by Dad M, who comes to sit in the middle of them on the sofa. Dad M has brown hair, it's messy with curls, and he is built like a giant. Their nicknames are based on their names, Mike, Pete, and Liam. I look at all three of them sitting there smiling. *Where's mum?*

"How's our little Kennie?" Dad M asks, leaning forward, so I can see his brown eyes in the camera.

"All good. Everything is—" I start to say, but I'm cut off.

"Don't try that with me. We can all tell when you're lying, Kennie and have done so since you were five, and you lied about who ate all the Smarties off your birthday cake, before your birthday. When were you going to tell us about your twelve marks?" Dad M says, narrowing his eyes on me in a way that tells me I'm in trouble. *Shit, who told him?*

I've been ignoring my brother's calls in case he tells

them, and they panic. One look at all their worried faces, and I know I was right not to tell them.

"I know it's a lot of marks, but come on, it's not that bad," I answer, and they all look at me like I'm stupid. *I might be.* I glance at the door as Kelly slides out of it and mouths 'later'. She's just abandoning me to my fate. I glare at her, which just makes her laugh as she leaves.

"Do you know how many marked I treat in the hospital that lose control of their powers and just about survive?" Dad P asks.

"Yes, Dad," I answer, and he continues on.

"Too many, and every goddamn day there is more. Our kind can't handle that amount of power without losing control, and I'm worried. I don't want to treat you for losing control or lose you altogether. So, you need to study and keep your emotions in check." *I don't know about my emotions, but my hormones need controlling around all the sexy guys here. Not that I'm going to enlighten any of my dads to that particular fact.*

"Yes, Mike is right, you need to focus," Dad P says, nodding just before my mum comes into view of the camera.

"Oh, Kennie, what trouble have you gotten yourself into now? I got a frantic call from your brother telling us about your marks. Everyone talking about you and how we could finally find out what the twelfth power is," she says as she sits on Dad P's lap.

"I don't know what it is. Mr. Daniels is doing classes with me, so I can learn," I say, deciding to use the word 'classes' and not 'detention'. *I don't need them freaking about that, too.*

"I want you to be careful, there has been—" my mum starts.

"That's enough, love," Dad M cuts her off.

"There's been what?" I ask, and they all look at each other.

"She should know, it's too much of a coincidence that this all started getting worse when she got her twelve powers," she says, and they all sigh. Her word is law with them. They rarely tell her no.

"The rebels have been getting stronger recently; more attacks, and more marked have been going missing," Dad M explains, running a hand through his curly hair.

"They killed one of the high council members and took something; we aren't sure what. I'm sure you will hear about it tomorrow around school, but I treated him. They killed twenty marked before they got to him. I don't know how they got so powerful or what they wanted, but I don't like it," Dad P says with a serious look. I know why he is worried. The high council members are the most powerful of our kind. All of them ten marks or eleven, and to beat one, you have to have some serious power. They were the ones with extreme power, but they also have the control to handle it, making them a force to be reckoned with.

"What could they possibly want?" I reply after a moment of silence.

"I don't know, Kennie, but train and stay safe. Watch your back, okay?" she answers with a serious look, and I nod. "And, call your brother," she adds, before she and the others say goodbye.

I turn the iPad off and reach for my phone on the side, every part of my body feeling like I've been run over from my torture earlier. I dial Ryan's number, and he answers on the third ring.

"Well, well, look who finally decided to call me back," the deep, sarcastic voice of my brother comes through the line.

"Don't be a little shit. I know you told our mum and dads about my marks," I say, and he laughs.

"Kennie, how did you expect to hide that?" he asks, and I hear the sounds of a chair creaking in the background.

"I don't know, but you know how they worry," I say.

"Shit, alright I'm sorry. How's the academy?" he asks, not sounding the least bit sorry.

"Full of drama, I can see why you didn't like it here. I just had detention, and I feel like death," I say.

"Who with?" he asks.

"Mr. Daniels," I say.

"Holy shit, that man is a god. Everyone knows about him and his family. His parents died protecting his sister, apparently," he says.

"Do you know much more?" I ask, wanting to know about him.

"No, but I feel sorry for his sister. I mean, I heard she joined the rebels because they want humans to know about us and so we don't have to hide. When the council found out, they tried to kill

CECE ROSE AND G. BAILEY

her, like they do all rebels, and her parents defended her," he says.

"Yeah, but the rebels don't just want the humans to find out. They want war, Ryan." I say, not liking how he is making them out to sound good. They aren't.

"Why is that so bad?" he asks. There's an awkward silence where I don't know how to respond, and he changes the subject. *I'm sure he didn't mean it.*

"Is Kelly okay? Has she met anyone?" he asks me.

"Why?" I ask.

"Just wondering, shit, can't I ask about your friend?" he says. Ryan has never asked about Kelly and ignored her a lot growing up, as much as he ignored me. The only time I saw them talk was last Christmas when Kelly came to dinner with us because her parents were out of town on business. Even then, it wasn't much more than a simple chat about something random on telly.

"Kelly is fine," I say slowly, and he clears his throat.

"How many marks did she get? I bet she got a lot," he asks.

"Two," I say

"Fuck, do her dads know?" he asks, reminding me that both her dads are part of London's council. There are twenty-four council members in each district, and there are five districts around the world. Her parents have an immense amount of power and growing up, they made it clear that they wanted Kelly to follow in their footsteps.

"No, they don't, but if they can't accept it . . . well they can go and fuck themselves," I say, and he laughs.

"Tell her, well I don't know, just that I said hello," he says, sounding awkward. *What the hell?*

"Right . . .," I say, trailing off.

"Gotta go, Kennie, later," Ryan quickly replies, and puts the phone down. I lie on my back on the bed and look up at the ceiling, coming to the conclusion that my brother is even weirder than I'd previously given him credit for being.

Chapter 14

LOCKE

"*W*hat class have you got now?" I ask Kenzie, outside my elective fighting class. Only East, Logan, and Enzo are in this class that Mr. Daniels teaches. All the others are too shit scared to try to fight us in here.

"Healing with Kelly. She is so excited," she replies.

"You best go," I say, nodding in the direction of her friend Kelly, who is walking towards us.

"See you later," she says, and I grab her arm gently.

"Don't I get a hug goodbye?" I say, and her cheeks go slightly red as she nods with a laugh. I pull her into a hug, loving the feel of her body pushed against mine, and kiss her cheek. As I pull my lips away and hear her little gasp, I see Mr. Daniels walking over to us. His eyes narrow on me and Kenzie. *What is that about?*

"You are going to be late for class, Miss Crowe," he says in a clipped tone as I let her go.

"Going, Mr. Daniels," she says, and I follow him into our class as Kenzie walks away.

I laugh as I watch East knock Logan on his ass with a blast of air as I take my coat off. They look like they have been at it a while. East walks over and offers him a hand up as Mr. Daniels starts clapping.

"Good. Locke, you're against me next," he says, and I internally groan. Logan pats my shoulder as he passes, and I walk in front of Mr. Daniels, quickly calling protection and shielding myself. He only smirks before jumping back and shifting mid-air into a large, grey wolf.

Guess I know what training he wants to do today. A neat trick is to have your protection ward on when you shift and your clothes stay with your human form. Thank the gods some mark figured that out, I don't want to see his naked ass.

I do the same, shifting into my own black panther, feeling the cold wash of my mark spreading all over my body. The shift is instant now, I only have to think about it, and I can shift. I remember how at the start, bonding with your chosen creature is difficult. Nearly impossible to control if it's strong. I ended up running around the forest for a whole day, trying to shift back. A loud growl is the only warning before Mr. Daniels' wolf slams into my side, biting my shoulder. I shake him off with a paw, scratching his side, and I snap my teeth at his leg, making him loosen his grip. I call my healing mark, as I step back, ignoring the blasting pain radiating through my back. *Fucking hell, he is serious today.*

Mr. Daniels shifts back suddenly, calling his water mark as I shift back. I'm too late as a wave of water surrounds me just as I get into my human form, and he uses his power to slam me into the wall. *Fucking hell, he used a lot of power to do that.*

"Very good. You almost got a hit in," he says, his words dripping with sarcasm. I stand up, looking around the room and seeing only East and Logan watching by the door.

"Almost seemed personal, sir," I say as he comes over, and I use air to dry my clothes. I remember the look he gave me when I kissed Kenzie's cheek. That was personal, and I know it as much as he does.

"This is training," he responds coldly.

"Nothing to do with a certain black-haired beauty, then?" I say, calling him out on that bullshit, and he narrows his eyes on me.

"Do you want detention?" he snaps.

"Would it be with Kenzie, sir? Because yes, yes I would," I say with a slow chuckle, and I swear I hear a slight growl from him. Mr. Daniels never loses any control, but when I look at him and see the slight glow of his eyes, I know he is close. *Seems the all-powerful teacher has a crush on a student, not that I can blame him.*

"Leave, now," he threatens, and I smirk.

"So soon?" I ask him, but he doesn't answer. "Shame you're her teacher, isn't it?" I add goadingly, and he growls louder as I leave. *Fuck it, I didn't want to go to his stupid class today, anyway.*

Chapter 15

KENZIE

"Come on, Kenz," Kelly urges, tugging me along. I cast a glance over my shoulder as we turn the corner, watching Mr. Daniels lead Locke into the classroom. From the look in Mr. Daniels eyes, I wouldn't want to be Locke right now. *I wonder what he did to provoke him? Whatever it is, I need to make a note to not do it.*

"I'm coming, I'm coming," I mumble, trusting Kelly to lead me in the right direction to class. She's a lot better at directions than I am, and she actually has her phone with her to use the map-app. That always helps.

"So, you and Locke looked close," she probes lightly.

"Nothing is going on, yet. You'd be the first to know, but I do like him," I admit.

"I think he likes you, if that kissing was anything to go by," she teases.

"Shut up! Totally doesn't count. Cheek. I kiss my mother on the cheek, hell, you kiss my mother on the cheek. What are you trying to say, that you're trying to bang my relatives?" I tease back. She flushes.

"Of course not. Ugh, come on, Kenz. We're running late. Have you been on time to any of your classes yet?" she asks.

"Um, maybe one?" I reply.

"Were you this bad in human school?" she asks.

"Worse," I answer with a grin. I think back on my time at the human, comprehensive school I went to in my home town. Most marked children get private tutors, or attend small marked schools, that teach the basic human subjects, Maths, English, and Science, as well as the history of the marked. My parents opted to send me to a human school, like Dad P went to. They taught me about marked history at home, not like I ever paid much attention. I always enjoyed human school, had human friends, and I loved some of my human classes. I think about some of my classes in particular, and my goals for when I left school. But now, it feels like my goals are never going to work, it feels like everything has changed. *The plan is still there, twelve marks or one. Three years at the marked academy, and then I can go back to the plan.* I think the mantra over in my head a few times. Maybe if I do that enough I can believe it.

I'm drawn out of my thoughts as we come to a stop outside of a classroom. Kelly pushes open the door, and I follow in after her. Everyone in the class is sitting at desks already, listening to our teacher. I inwardly groan as all the eyes turn to me and Kelly.

"Sorry we're late, sir," Kelly says, giving him her sweetest look. Like everyone else does when Kelly uses that look, the teacher's frown fades away, and he smiles back at her.

"That is fine, Miss Curwood. Please can you and Miss Crowe take a seat?"

I try to spot where we can sit, but there aren't any seats together. Kelly slips into a spare seat in the front, next to a guy with pale-blond hair. I glance around for another empty seat. *You have got to be kidding me? Ugh.* I make my way across the room and drop into the only free seat left, which just so happens to be next to Enzo. Sighing as I shove my bag under the desk, I deliberately face forward, pointedly ignoring him.

"You look pleased to see me," he mutters.

"Because it's always such a pleasure to see you," I chirp back sarcastically.

"You are so frustrating. I can't believe I'm missing my elective with Mr. Daniels for this," he says bitterly.

"I didn't ask you to," I snap back.

"No, because if you did, I'd have told you where to go. I'm here because Mr. Daniels asked me to be. That's it," he says sharply, and a little too loudly. A couple of students sitting around us shoot dark looks in our direction. I kick Enzo's foot under the table.

"Shut up," I mutter. He kicks my foot back. *Asshole isn't meant to kick me back!* I kick his shin this time, harder and shoot a smug look at him. *Like he's going to —Ouch! The fucker actually kicked me harder.*

"Don't start what you can't finish, Crowe," he snaps.

"Who said I won't," I reply, narrowing my eyes on him.

"Important conversation you're having I assume, Miss Crowe, Mr. Langston?" the teacher asks, somehow having snuck right up to our desk. *I wonder why Enzo has a different surname to his sister? Did he not take his mum's name, or did she not?*

"No, sir," Enzo says quickly. I follow suit and shake my head.

"Well, I will assume the two of you were listening and know exactly what we are doing today then?" he asks.

"Yes, sir," we both answer in unison. A united front in our joint lie at least.

"Good. Everyone stand up and get into pairs for the activity," he instructs as he walks back towards his desk. I quickly move from my seat and grab Kelly.

"What are we doing?" I whisper to her.

"We're meant to be reading each other for injury or sickness," she whispers back.

"How are we meant to—"

"Miss Curwood, Crowe, you two girls first," the teacher calls, cutting me off. *Shit.* He gestures for the two of us to come to the front of the classroom. The smug look on his rounded face telling me that he knows I have no clue what I'm doing, and has just called me up to humiliate me. *I thought healers were meant to be gentle, kind souls.* I roll my eyes and saunter up to the front of the class with Kells in tow. *It's cool, I'll just copy Kelly.*

"Miss Crowe, you will check Miss Curwood first," he instructs.

Well, there goes that plan . . . how the heck did Mr. Daniels check me for injuries? Hand on forehead? I never realised how inconvenient my never getting sick would be. The sound of a throat clearing makes me jump.

"Anytime now, Miss Crowe," he says, sighing with exasperation.

I lay a hand across Kelly's forehead and close my eyes, trying to concentrate. I picture the healing mark. *Nothing. Shit.* I open my eyes and move my hand from her head, stepping back.

"She's all good," I announce.

"Are you sure about that?" he asks sceptically.

"Yep, I'm feeling great, sir," Kelly answers for me.

"Fine, Curwood, your turn," he says curtly, shooting me a disbelieving look, but it's not like he can just call me a liar in front of the whole class. I'd look up how to do it later.

Kelly places a hand over my forehead and closes her eyes. I feel the light, probing feeling roll through me. *Trust Kelly to get it right first time.* She drops her hand and her eyes fly open.

"You're hurt," she accuses.

"It's nothing much," I mutter back. *Just an aching all over my body that won't go away since bitchface Stella zapped me.* She frowns and puts her hands either side of my head and closes her eyes again.

"Wait, Miss Curwood, you really should not be doing that," the teacher begins to say, when suddenly, a glow takes over Kelly, much like when she had the vision. *Shit.* A hush falls over the room.

I'm about to move back from her hold on my head, when a feeling of lightness fills me. I feel like every inch of my body is sparking for a moment, and then nothing. I feel fine, the aching is gone. A rush of energy hits me.

"Shit, Kells. I feel like new," I mumble, feeling like I could climb a mountain or run a marathon right now. She moves her hand.

"S-sorry," she stutters to the teacher. "I just knew I could do it," she says simply. He stares at her for a moment like she's this peculiar creature, and he just doesn't know what to do with her.

"Take your seats, both of you," he says. We quickly scarper back into some seats, she slips into what was Enzo's seat to stay with me. After a tense moment or so, the teacher calls the attention back to the front of the class, and calls up another two students.

"What the hell was that, Kells?" I ask her, feeling a little concerned.

"I have no idea, Kenz. Not a fucking clue."

Chapter 16

KENZIE

*a*s I walk into my next class, I inwardly groan when I spot the person who will be my extra help in this class. Stella is sitting at the back of the classroom, a satisfied smile on her face. *Of course, Stella would be the one to volunteer to be in my pain class. Just freaking typical.*

As I've managed to arrive late, again, there are no spare seats apart from right next to her. *The universe hates me, I am sure of it.* I glumly walk across the classroom and take my seat next to her without saying so much as a word. I look up to try and spot the teacher, seeing that they haven't arrived yet. *Huh, a teacher that shows up late, finally some luck.*

Everyone is chatting, or on their phones. I reach into my bag for my own phone, glad I stopped by my dorm at lunch for it. I notice a couple texts from my brother. I frown and then open them, surprised by getting a message at all when we only talked on the phone last night.

Ryan: I heard something happened with Kelly in her classes? Something about glowing. Can you let me know what is up?

Ryan: Kennie, stop being so shit at replying and answer your phone.

Ryan: I swear there is no point in you owning a phone sometimes.

I can't help but smile a little at his frustration, knowing that my rejection of technology is a constant source of annoyance to my family. I go to reply, then I hear the door to the classroom loudly slam shut. I drop my phone, it hits the floor with a crack. Shit. I quickly pick it up and assess the damage. *Fuck's sake.* A large crack runs right down the centre of the screen, several little cracks running off it. I can't help but think that the shattered phone screen resembles the cracks on the arrow-struck circle of the twelfth mark. I tuck it back into my bag sorrowfully, I've had that phone for six years. *I guess I'll finally need to upgrade.*

I jump again at the sound of something loud crashing down onto a table. I look up and see the teacher has loudly slammed a pile of books onto their desk. I gulp. *There goes thinking I was maybe in luck with this teacher.*

The teacher has long, black hair tied back in a low

ponytail, pale-white, almost translucent looking skin, sharp features, and dark eyes that look like deep pools of nothingness. He's tall and slim, but still somehow appears intimidating despite not having a broad frame. The look on his face is pure annoyance. *Who the heck saw this guy and thought, 'yep that's the one, let's hire him and give all the students nightmares?'* I shudder at the thought of this guy slipping into my nightmares, already feeling like he'll be scary enough to handle in these lessons.

He looks around the room, pausing when he looks in my direction. *Crap, what now?*

"Stella, what are you doing in this class? You passed all three years of pain already," he says, his voice is low and unpleasant. I turn to Stella, relieved it wasn't actually me he was looking at.

"I know, it's ridiculous, Uncle," she responds, rolling her eyes. She jabs a finger to point at me. "I'm here to babysit this one, someone thinks she might have a little too much juice to play nicely with the other first years, but I've seen no evidence of that." She huffs, and leans back in her chair, a look of annoyance that mirrors the teacher's painted across her face, but her eyes hold a scheming edge. I flush, feeling every student in the room's eyes on me.

"You are?" he asks me.

"Mackenzie Crowe," I tell him, and he narrows his eyes at me and walks to the front of the class.

"I'm Mr. Tower, and welcome to pain class," he says in a bored tone as he leans against his desk. "Pain is one of our strongest marks and one many people

CECE ROSE AND G. BAILEY

overlook because you cannot see it. The pain mark is very difficult to block and difficult to have any control over. I'm here to teach you control and how to use pain, without accidentally killing someone," he explains, his tone sounding like he has repeated the same sentence a million times.

"Did you like the pain mark, Mackenzie?" Stella asks with a chuckle, and I glare at her.

"Fuck off," I reply and turn back to look at Mr. Tower as he looks around the class.

"To use your pain mark is simple, you just imagine the mark and then the amount of pain you wish to cause that person. If you wish to kill them, you can. If you wish to paralyze them, you can," he says and carries on listing as Stella whispers.

"I could have killed you, you know that, right?" I don't reply or even bother looking at her as she speaks. "Stay the fuck away from Enzo and East, or I will kill you little *Mac-ken-zie*. The twelfth mark will be useless to protect you," she says in a sweet tone, the tone is creepy as hell considering it's laced with threat at the same time. I go to reply then I hear Mr. Tower speak louder.

"What's your name?" he asks a blond guy in the front row.

"Sam Pagan," the guy replies. Mr. Tower waves him over and straightens up off the desk. Sam stops in front of him, and Mr. Tower holds an arm out.

"Place your hand on mine and use your pain mark," Mr. Tower says, and I lean forward on my desk to watch. Sam nods and does it. I wait for any reaction from Mr. Tower, but there isn't any. Suddenly, Sam screams out, dropping to the floor. Mr. Tower grins sardonically, looking pleased with himself and making no move to help Sam up. *What the hell was that?*

"Pain is easy to stop and send back, as Mr. Pagan has just learnt. Another volunteer?" he asks, and there's silence around the room. *Who would be crazy enough to go up there?*

"Uncle, Mackenzie just said she wants to volunteer," Stella shouts out, and I narrow my eyes at her. *Just friggin great.*

"Both of you come up here," Mr. Tower says, and Stella's smirk only grows. *She planned this.* I slide out of my seat and walk to the front of the class, watching as Sam walks slowly back to his seat and gives me a worried look. I pull my eyes away from him and force myself to remember the protection mark Mr. Daniels' taught me as I stand next to Stella.

"Now, I don't expect you to use your full power, Stella," he says and Stella chuckles, mumbling something I can't hear, and likely don't want to. "But, I expect you to show Kenzie how strong pain can be. Kenzie, I want you to *try* and use your pain mark against Stella," he directs us, clearly thinking I don't have a chance as he nods at me. Stella holds a hand out, and I call my protection mark, imagining it covering me and then picture my pain mark, the two seem to work well together in my mind, but I have no idea if this will work until I take her hand.

I force myself to forget the pain she made me feel at the party and place my hand in hers. There's a slight wave of pain that shoots up my arm, but I concentrate, pushing the pain mark into my mind and imagining it hurting her. I glance up to see her eyes widen, seconds before she starts screaming and trying to pull her hand away, but I don't want to let go. All I can remember is her threatening to kill me. To hurt me like she did before.

"Kenzie, stop this now," Mr. Tower shouts, but I don't see anything other than Stella screaming and the pain mark in my mind. I briefly imagine the twelfth mark, the arrow and the broken sphere, and I start feeling the mark burning on the back of my neck just before everything goes black.

"KENZIE," East's voice says gently as I blink my eyes open. East is holding me on his lap, my head on his shoulder and his hand wrapped around my hip.

"What happened?" I ask, looking around the room and seeing that we are in my bedroom, sitting on my bed. The curtains are open and the room is tidy. *Thank gods, I cleaned up my underwear from the floor this morning.*

"Mr. Tower had to knock you out when you used too much pain on Stella. You nearly killed her, Kenz," he says gently, and I remember it. I couldn't stop myself, and it felt like the mark was taking me over.

"Don't worry. Some powers are harder to control, and pain is addictive. I have that mark," he tells me, and I rest my head back on his shoulder. I feel safe around East, and I'm thankful it was him that found me. I glance down at his soft-blue shirt, and his tight jeans. *He is looking as sexy as ever.*

"I couldn't stop, and then I pictured the twelfth mark . . .," I say and stop talking. The mark just popped into my mind, pushing out the pain mark, but she was still screaming. So I must have still been hurting her. Everything is blurry, but I couldn't have been holding her for more than a couple of minutes, or Mr. Tower would have stopped me sooner.

"The room shook, just before he knocked you out. I was walking past and ran in," he says gently, moving to stroke my forehead. I stay still as I feel his hand get warm. *He's healing me.*

"The room shook?" I ask when he pulls his hand away. I move a little and become very aware that I'm on his lap, all alone in my room. I try not to blush as he speaks, his voice is so seductive and he doesn't know it.

"Yes, like an earthquake, but it was no earth power," he replies. I nod, still a little speechless, and now I can't think about the pain class at all. *Sexy East is in my bed, holding me. Kelly is never going to believe this.*

"Why are we in my room, and why am I in your lap?" I ask, and he chuckles.

"Don't you like being on my lap?" he asks me, his tone dropping and his voice becoming even more seductive. I move my head up in confusion, wondering why he would flirt with me. A stray lock of his blond-tipped hair falls into his eyes, and as I reach up to push it out of the way, East meets my eyes. His gaze is full of desire, something I never thought I'd see directed at me. East has never looked at me like this before.

"East–" I start to say, and he kisses me. I freeze for a second, in shock, and then I respond by gently kissing him back. East's hand slides into my hair as he deepens the kiss, the kiss is so powerful that I can't think straight until he pulls away. *Sexy East kissed me.*

"Shit! I shouldn't have done that," he says in a gruff tone, moving me off his lap and standing up off the bed.

"Why? You wanted it as much as did," I say, ignoring the trickle of doubt that comes into my mind. *Did he not like the kiss?*

"Ryan will go crazy. You're his little sister, and —" he starts, and I cut him off, not willing to listen to excuses.

"Just leave," I say, gesturing at the door. He stares down at me, not moving.

"Kenz," he starts again, and I stand up, crossing the room and holding the door open for him.

"I've always liked you, East, but if you're not prepared to be with me because of your friendship with my brother, then I'm not chasing you like all the girls I knew growing up, did. I'm not one of those girls, no matter how much I liked that kiss," I say, and he chuckles, then it stops, and his eyes widen.

"Shit, you always liked me?" he asks, walking over and using that seductive voice again. I don't breathe as he stops in front of me, so close that all I can do is look up at him. I know he can see how upset I am, and I hate that, I don't want him to know he affects me.

"Always," I answer, and he leans forward, kissing me gently, and then stepping back.

"I've got to call your brother," he says with a little cheeky grin, but I know he is worried.

"East, are you sure?" I ask, and he nods.

"I want to date you, and I can't do that if I'm lying to him. So, I'm going to tell him, and then I'm taking you out on a real date," he says, making me blush.

"And, how do you know I'm going to say yes to that date?" I ask, and he chuckles slowly as his eyes rake all over my body before finally landing on my eyes.

"Kenz, I know you'll say yes," he replies confidently, before walking out of my room. I want to say no, but as I glance at his jean-covered ass as he walks away, I know I'll say yes too.

Chapter 17

LOGAN

"Yes . . . I kissed her," East says as I walk into our room. I pull my coat off and leave my phone on the side. I give him a questioning look as he listens to someone else on the phone. I can hear them shouting from here, and East is slightly holding the phone away from his ear.

"No. Look, calm down and call me back when you're being more reasonable," East says and stops the call. I know that voice, it's Ryan.

"Kenzie?" I ask, holding in the jealously I feel when he nods. I saw the way she looked at him, and the way she looks at me, sometimes. Females are rarer than males in our kind and it can be difficult for a female marked to have children, so more than one husband is recommended. My mum has three husbands, they all brought me up, and I call them all dad. It may not be a lifestyle for humans, but it works

120

for us. I could share Kenzie with East. *If she likes me, that is.*

"How was it?" I ask, and he smirks at me.

"Why don't you find out for yourself? I know that look, dickhead," he says, and I laugh and jump on my bed, quickly stretching out.

"What happened in pain?" I ask him, having heard about what happened in the halls just then, and hearing that East stormed off carrying Kenzie, telling the teacher to go fuck himself and speak to Mr. Daniels if he had a problem. I bet that shut him up quick.

"She lost it and nearly killed Stella. I didn't want to freak her out, so I didn't tell her everything that happened when I got there."

"What happened? I heard rumours about some kind of black glow?" I ask. It sounded like bullshit to me.

"Kenz was glowing with like a black haze around her, and there was a force pushing everyone away from her. Mr. Tower used air to throw her across the room, and I just about managed to catch her," he says. *Fucking hell.* When Mr. Daniels asked us to watch her, he warned that it might be dangerous as we have no clue what her twelfth mark is. I've never heard of anyone glowing black before or being able to create a force that pushes people away, other than just using air, but this wasn't anything like an air mark. There was no gust of wind, just an intense pressure that forced people back. *I wonder what the hell that last power is?*

I know it's something powerful because I asked one of my dads who works at the Marked History Museum. Apparently, there is a book about the twelfth mark, and all the book talks about is destroying those that have the mark. I don't see how Kenzie could be a threat, and that's only one crazy, dead person's opinion, but this won't help her case.

"Did she pass out?" I ask.

"Yeah, she did," he replies, picking his phone up as it starts ringing. "Calmed down yet, dickhead?" East mutters as he answers the phone. His eyes widen. "Shit, sorry, mum, thought it was someone else calling." He shoots me a grin and rolls his eyes. I can hear his mum's scolding down the phone from the other side of the room.

My own phone starts to buzz, and I look down. Fuck.

"Hey, Ryan," I answer loudly, so that East can hear. He shoots me a worried look. He's clearly much more concerned by whatever Ryan has to say than his mother's yelling.

"Put East on the phone," Ryan grunts.

"Can't, he's on the phone to his mum," I reply.

"Fuck his mum!" Ryan shouts.

"Calm down Ry, he can't go fucking his mum just because he's screwing your sister," I joke.

"I'm not screwing anyone," East yells across the room, clearly hoping Ryan will hear him. "Sorry, mum, again," he says down the phone, a pained expression crossing his face.

"You know what I meant. Tell East he's not dating my fucking sister, okay?" he snaps.

"Yeah, sure. I'll pass on the message, but what about me?" I slip in.

"You have got to be kidding me," he mutters.

"No, I'm not kidding, Ry," I reply.

"She's my little sister," he growls.

"She's really not that little anymore. It's not really your decision either way. East asking you was a courtesy, but I know that I am still going to pursue her either way, and so will he," I say calmly.

"I'm not happy about this," he mutters. "Kennie needs to be concentrating right now."

"Who are you now, her dad?" I jibe.

"Depends which one," he answers with a harsh laugh. "She's got twelve powers, she needs to concentrate. I don't want her being one of those people who lose control," he says softly.

"We won't distract her. We're helping her in her classes, anyway, dude. We care about Kenzie. We won't do anything that puts her in danger."

"I guess. Better the devil you know, right?" he comments, sighing in defeat. "Look, I'm not happy, but I guess I can't stop you. Just know I won't hesitate to kill any of you if you hurt her," he mutters.

"We got it, dude," I reply. I shoot a thumbs up to East, who grins back at me like a maniac.

"Tell East I still want to talk to him. There's things I want to make clear to him, especially considering his track record," Ryan mutters.

"Sure, I'll tell him."

"Thanks, mate. I've got to go," he says.

"Okay, bye, then."

"Bye," he says, and then the call disconnects.

"So," East says, dragging out the word.

"I thought you were on the phone to your mum?" I ask, narrowing my eyes on him.

"The call disconnected about a minute ago, bad reception where she is I guess," he says shrugging.

"You were still talking," I accuse him.

He smiles slyly. "Yeah, I really didn't fancy talking to Ryan. Thanks for sorting that out for me," he replies.

"Ryan still wants to talk to you about it," I say, watching the smile fade from his face.

"Damn," he says softly.

"Not off the hook that easy," I reply with a chuckle.

"I have a feeling nothing about Kenzie is going to be easy," he replies, a smile taking over his face in contradiction to his words. "But, when was easy ever fun?" he adds, standing up.

"Where are you going?" I ask, watching him saunter off to the door.

"Where do you think?" he replies as he exits the room, slamming the door behind him.

Chapter 18

KENZIE

I sink deeper into the tub, feeling the hot water work out all the knots in my body as I relax, breathing in the aroma from the bath bombs I'd thrown in. *I'm sure Kelly won't mind the fact I nicked a few.* The purple, bubble-covered hot water is heavenly, and I'm making no attempt to move anytime soon. I shut my eyes and just relax, listening to the soft music I'd left playing in my room carry through the door into the bathroom. *Peace.*

I'm jarred awake by the sound of the bathroom door crashing open. I sit up, crossing a hand over my chest as I face the person who'd let themselves in.

"Shit, Kenz," East exclaims, staring right at me, where I'm sitting, naked, in the bathtub.

"What the hell are you doing in here?" I all but screech, feeling mortified. Sexy East kisses me, and then walks in on me naked in the bathtub all in one day. Kelly was never going to believe this.

"You didn't answer when I called, I thought . . . I thought maybe something had happened, okay?" he says quickly, stepping back. I am so thankful for all the bubbles right now, at least they are affording me some coverage.

"I fell asleep. I didn't hear you," I explain, shrinking back down lower into the tub, hoping to hide more of myself.

"Why is your door open? Kenz are you okay?" Locke's voice comes from the bedroom, just seconds before he walks into the bathroom, and his eyes widen. He looks between me and East, then smirks.

"Move out of the way, why are you just standing there?" Logan's voice comes from behind Locke, and I meet his eyes over his twin's shoulder. He looks just as shocked.

"Out, all of you," I say, and Locke laughs slightly, his eyes running over my body in the water. I don't think he can see me, but his grin suggests otherwise. I sink myself as low as possible in the water, praying the purple bubbles hide me. I mean, three extremely hot men are in my bathroom, while I'm naked. I didn't know if this was a gift or punishment from the gods.

"But, you let East in here," Locke whines playfully, and East grabs his arm, dragging him from the room. Logan grabs the door, giving me a small smile as he follows after them. I wait until the door is shut before getting out of the bath. *There goes my plan to relax in the bath for an hour.* I dry myself off and mentally curse when I realise I've not brought any clothes in here with me. I tighten my towel around myself before opening the door a little and leaning out.

"Logan?" I ask.

"Yes," he answers, getting off the chair he was sitting in and walking over. East and Locke watch as they both sit on my bed.

"Could you get me some clothes?" I ask him.

"I can get your underwear," Locke says with a big grin, and I glare at him.

"No . . . Logan can," I reply, and Logan chuckles, but starts moving around my room getting things. He comes back and passes me a bundle of clothes through the door, keeping his eyes on mine, and I kind of like that he does that. I laugh a little when I see he has chosen my lacy, red bra and matching, red knickers. *Maybe Logan likes me in red?* I'm glad I chose Logan when I see my tight, skinny jeans and grey jumper in the pile. I pull them all on and plait my towel-dried hair, just before the academy shakes, and I fall to the ground, my back slamming into the bath tub as I slide across the floor.

"Get Kenz," I hear East shout as the shaking stops, and I stand up as Locke opens the door.

"You okay?" he asks me as he rushes in, and I nod. He takes my hand, leading me back into the bedroom where East and Logan are waiting. The room is a mess, the wardrobe is on the floor, and my stuff is all over the place. I step over my upside-down basket and pick up my iPad, the screen is cracked, and it's far worse than my phone. *Great, just friggin great.*

"What was that?" I ask, but no one answers as a message fills the room, it takes me a minute to realise that there must be hidden speakers.

"The Academy is under attack, please stay in your rooms. If anyone is hurt, report to the gym once lockdown is over." The message cuts out, and the room is silent for a second.

"Attacked by the rogues?" I ask as Logan slams the bedroom door shut.

"They have been attacking places recently, they must want something from here," East says and looks at me strangely. My phone starts ringing, and I look around, finding it on the floor by the bed. I just about manage to unlock the phone with the cracked screen.

"Kenz, I'm in the library, and we are trapped. They are breaking all the boxes in here, and I'm hiding. Are you safe?" Kelly says, and I go to reply, when my phone beeps before turning off.

"Kelly? Kelly, no," I say, trying to turn the phone back on. *Stupid phone.* I don't think as I walk towards the door and pull it open, ignoring the guys shouting for me as I run down the corridor and towards the library.

"Kenz, don't!" East shouts as I run down the stairs. I rush out into the courtyard and across into the main building, hearing the guys chase after me. Other than me and the guys, there is no one around, and there's a loud noise coming from the direction of the library when I get to it. *Where are the teachers?* I run around the corridor, seeing the doors to the library, and there is a girl standing outside. The girl has on a leather jacket, leather trousers, and has long, brown hair up in a ponytail. She smiles widely when she sees me, and she looks familiar as her green eyes look over at me. A scream comes from the library, and I step forward, stopping when I see the student at her feet. He looks familiar and must be from one of my classes. He is withering in pain as she places her hand on his forehead. She's using pain on him, and a lot of it.

"Little girl, you might want to turn around," she says, moving her hand, and the guy passes out.

"No," I say coldly, hearing East, Locke, and Logan as they come to my side. I look at them briefly, and Locke glares at me, but doesn't say anything. All of them seem to be at the same conclusion as me, I'm not leaving without Kelly. She doesn't have defensive powers.

"This should be fun," the girl laughs as she raises her hands, and a gust of air slams into us. I hold my hands up, calling my own air power, but all I do is manage to stop myself from flying. It doesn't matter as Locke wraps his arm around my waist and lifts his hand, making a white ward appear. It's shaped like a shield, and it stops the wind from getting to us. I turn and watch as East flies up into the air, lifting his hands, and Logan uses a stream of water which he pushes against the wind, mixing with it. He shoots the jet of water straight at the girl. He does it so fast that she can't move in time, and the water makes her slam into the corridor wall. The girl stands up with a little smirk and shifts. I've never seen a shift before, none of my parents have that mark. It's like her body glimmers a little and goes blurry as her shape changes. I step back when I see the giant snake she has turned into. The snake is green and massive, bigger than a car.

"Gods . . .," I say, my voice trailing off as I watch. Locke lowers his hand, the shield disappearing. He pulls me closer to his side as Logan steps in front of us, and East literally flies and lands next to him.

"We have to go," a man says running out of the library and stopping in front of the snake girl. The man is older, with black hair and wearing a black cloak with the hood down. He is holding a blue box, which looks old and covered in marks. He seems to realise we are all looking at him as he turns and lifts his hands. A white ward spreads from his hands, until there's a wall between us and them.

"Stop playing with the kids, I got it," the man says holding up the box, and the snake turns, slithering down the corridor. The man looks back at me once as I push between Logan and East. He doesn't say anything, but he gives me a strange look, like he knows me before pulling his hood up. I watch as he turns and runs off after the snake.

"Can we break the ward?" I ask after they both disappear. *I need to get to Kelly.*

"Yes, we can do it together. I'm the only one out of us guys with the ward power, but between us two, we can overload it," Locke tells me. He takes my hand and walks us up to the ward.

"Imagine the ward cracking, breaking into tiny parts and call your protection mark into your mind, Kenz," he tells me and I nod, doing as he asks as he places our joined hands on the ward. I close my eyes as I feel the power from it spread down my arm, it's slightly painful. I imagine it breaking, and falling into little, white bits. When I open my eyes, Locke is smiling down at me and all around us are little bits of the ward. It's like snow falling, and we lower our hands.

"Kenzie," Kelly shouts, and I turn to see her running out of the library. She throws herself into my arms, and I wrap my arms around her and hug her tightly. *Thank Gods she is okay.*

"What happened?" I ask, but she doesn't get a chance to reply as I hear Mr. Daniels shout behind us.

"What are you doing out of your rooms?"

I turn to see him storming down the corridor, and aiming straight for me as Kelly steps away. He looks angry, and it's a bit scary. It's also a good look on him, it's hot.

"Kelly called, and I–" I get out before he interrupts.

"No. I don't care. Do you not realise what they wanted, Miss Crowe? How much danger you were in?" he snaps. I take a step back, surprised he would speak to me like that. I'm not stupid, and I know how dangerous it was running here, but I would never forgive myself if Kelly died while I sat in my room hiding. *That's not me.*

"Don't speak to her like that," East says protectively, and it seems to make Mr. Daniels even madder. East comes to my side and links his fingers with mine.

"You all have detention, and get to your goddamn rooms now!" he shouts, his voice echoing down the corridor. The guys all glare at him but start to walk away with Kelly following. East tugs on my hand, and we start to follow Kelly.

"Not you, Miss Crowe, the headteachers want to see you. Now," Mr. Daniels says.

"Fine," I say stopping.

"Good luck," East whispers to me and squeezes my hand before walking off with Kelly. Locke and Logan shoot me worried glances as they go up the stairs.

"Let's go then," I say, walking away from him and towards the stairs.

"Fuck, wait," Mr. Daniels says, catching up to me and grabbing my arm to stop me.

"Why? Do you want to shout at me more for trying to save my friend? I'm not saying sorry for it," I tell him, he looks down at me, and then to his hand on my arm. He doesn't move his hand like I expect him to.

"I'm sorry. I was scared you were hurt. I went to your room, looking for you and panicked when you weren't there," he tells me softly. I move my hand, placing it on his chest before I say anything. I'm surprised he doesn't stop me, and I can feel his heart beating fast under my palm.

"I'm okay," I tell him gently, watching as his eyes search my own.

"Mackenzie," he says my name slowly as he moves closer, and his hand slides up my arm.

"Mr. Daniels," a voice shouts down the corridor,

and he jumps away from me. *What the hell just happened between us?* I turn to see Miss Tinder walking towards us from the stairs. She doesn't look impressed and flashes me a disgusted look. I try not to chuckle when I see her red hair is now short, cut into a bob, and I know it's because of our lesson. *Serves her right.*

"Mr. Daniels, the headteachers are waiting for Miss Crowe, and you are needed in the gym. We have caught some of the rogues, and we need you to make them shift back," she says. I didn't know he could do that. I know that it's a sign that his transmutation mark is extremely strong and makes him an alpha over most animals. *I wonder what he shifts into?*

"No problem," he says and walks away. I watch as he looks back at me once, a confused look in his eyes, and I know it's not just me that felt something then. These kinds of feelings could get him fired and me kicked out of the academy. As much as I like him, I don't want that for him or me.

"Come now, Miss Crowe," Miss Tinder says, and I follow her down the stairs, feeling sad that I didn't meet Mr. Daniels somewhere else.

Chapter 19

KENZIE

I've been at The Marked Academy less than a week, and somehow this is my second visit inside the headmasters' office. *Just my luck.* I tap my fingers against my knees, and glance over my shoulder every so often, waiting for someone to join me in the room. However, they appear to be letting me stew.

I don't see why I should be in trouble, I was just trying to help my friend. Surely, they should understand that? And, it's not like I was the only one out of their room. They just don't like me, that's gotta be it. The sound of the door opening behind me cuts off my inner rambling.

I turn around and watch as all three headmasters of the school enter the office, followed by Mr. Daniels. *I swear that man is everywhere.* One of the headmasters takes the seat behind the desk I'm facing toward. The other two push their chairs over as well, either side of him, so they are all facing across from me. One united front against Kenzie. *Because that's not intimidating at all.* A chair scrapes against the floor next to me, I turn my head and notice Mr. Daniels sitting beside me. A warm feeling runs through me as he shoots me a reassuring smile.

"Miss Crowe, what on Ariziadia were you thinking?" one of the headmasters, Mr. Lockhart, asks.

"She wasn't thinking, clearly," the headmaster to the left, Mr. Layan, adds.

"Hey!" I exclaim, lurching forward slightly in my seat. A hand rests on my forearm, reminding me to keep calm. I sit back in my seat and glare at the men across from me. "I was just—"

"Being foolish?" The third headmaster, who's name I can't remember, says cutting me off.

"That's not fair, let me explain," I reply, trying to curb the whine in my voice. *This fucking sucks.*

"Life isn't fair, Miss Crowe. Just because you have twelve marks, don't expect life to give you special treatment," Mr. Layan says, flicking a strand of his blond hair from his face.

"I'm not expecting special treatment, I'm asking for fair treatment," I mutter, but he catches it.

"Are you talking back to me?" Mr. Layan questions, glaring at me.

"I'm sure Miss Crowe didn't mean to, did you?" Mr. Daniels says softly, drawing the focus to himself. "Miss Crowe, if you would please listen to the headmasters, they do have concerns they wish to explain. I'm sure

CECE ROSE AND G. BAILEY

they were just about to get to the point?" he says, his tone laced with bite at the last part directed at the three headmasters, none of which dare to call him on it.

"Yes, yes. Miss Crowe, the people who attacked the school are members of a marked terrorist group. I'm not sure how much of this you have heard about, but they seek to start a revolution, one that would be very dangerous for both humans and our own kind," Mr. Lockhart explains.

"I've heard of them, but why would they come to the academy?" I ask.

"The intelligence we were sent from the council indicates they came for two things. One of which they succeeded in getting, and the other which they failed to collect," Mr. Lockhart answers.

"What things?" I question.

"One was a necklace, an artifact we believe came across from Ariziadia. It's believed to strengthen the twelfth power," the other headmaster answers, giving me a pointed look. I swallow and look between the four men in the room, already knowing the answer but needing to ask all the same.

"And, the other?" I whisper.

"They were after you, Miss Crowe," Mr. Daniels answers, the seriousness in his low voice sending a shiver through me. I'm silent for a moment, but then a thought strikes me.

"Wait a minute, does that mean they would have gone looking for me? Gone to my dorm room?" I question.

"Well—" Mr. Layan begins, but I cut him off.

"So, you're telling me off for leaving my room, which I would have been kidnapped from if I stayed put?" I question, not able to stop the snarky tone slipping into my voice.

"Mr. Daniels was instructed to collect you if and when an attack happened. He has a copy of your full timetable, and any regular movements of yours are made known to him. You weren't where you were meant to be."

"You're spying on me?" I ask as I turn to the side to face Mr. Daniels.

"Only to keep you safe. Since you were marked last week, there have been a lot of stirrings from the group. They want you. I'm not sure if it's your power or for the show of power, but they do."

"But, I don't understand, you're acting like you knew about this for longer?" I question. He sighs and runs a hand through his hair before answering.

"A gifted seer predicted a student would be given twelve marks. I've been here under order from the council for the past two years waiting. They wanted me to stay teaching in the school, so it would not look suspicious when the student with twelve did start," he explains.

"You're not really a teacher?" I ask.

"I am. Well, now I am anyway. But, my main job is to keep you safe," he says. He turns and directs his attention to the headmasters. "I do not think Miss Crowe should be staying in the dorm any longer. It's not safe, I need to be able to keep a closer eye on her, while not interrupting her studies."

"What are you suggesting?" Mr. Lockhart asks, raising a thick, dark eyebrow in question.

"I think she should stay with me, I have a spare room. Then she would either be with me, in the main building, or attending a lesson," he says. *Stay with Mr. Daniels? He cannot be serious.*

"I really don't think this would be wise," Mr. Lockhart says, narrowing his eyes on me, as if Mr. Daniels' insane suggestion was my fault.

"I agree,"

"It's not a suggestion Mr. Kane," Mr. Daniels replies, finally reminding me of the third headmaster's name.

"You can't just — "

"Am I really going to have to call down to London and get them to overrule you?" Mr. Daniels asks, cutting Mr. Kane off.

Identical looks of annoyance cross all three headmasters' faces, clearly unhappy with the fact that he could so easily go over their heads.

"Of course not. If this is the best way to keep Miss Crowe safe, then by all means, she may stay with you," Mr. Lockhart says, his voice suggesting the very opposite of his agreeing statement.

"I do think it would be best," Mr. Daniels replies, standing to leave. "Come along, Miss Crowe." I stand and turn around to follow him, not giving the headmasters another look either. *They clearly aren't in charge here.*

"Do I get a say in this?" I mutter as we exit the office.

"Not a damn word, Miss Crowe," he replies without humour, and continues down the corridor, not waiting for me to catch up.

Chapter 20

KENZIE

$\mathcal{I}$ try to avoid the looks I get from the other students as I walk into the dining hall for breakfast. Making a beeline for where Kelly, East, and the twins are sitting, not even detouring to get food or coffee. I slump down into the seat next to Kelly.

"You look tired, I'm guessing you didn't get any sleep after what happened last night then?" East asks from across the table.

"I look tired? Everyone knows that's polite code for you look like crap," I mutter, snagging a piece of toast from Logan's plate. He frowns but doesn't say anything as I munch silently, avoiding the looks of everyone else in the room.

"Fine, you look crappy, is that what you wanted to hear?" Kelly chimes in sarcastically. "I'm worried, why did they move you?" she asks.

"Isn't it obvious?" Locke says, answering for me. Kelly shakes her head, clearly confused.

"The rogues were after her," Logan answers.

"What?! You can't be serious," Kelly says, shooting me a concerned look before focusing her gaze back on the twins. "How would you know?" They both shrug in sync.

"It's obvious, why else would they move Kenzie?" East says.

"Well clearly, it's obvious to everyone but me," Kelly says, sighing. "I was so worried when someone came in and grabbed all your stuff last night, Kenz," she adds. I grab for her hand and give her my best attempt at a reassuring smile.

"It's fine, honestly," I say softly.

"Where are you staying now? Somewhere safer?" she asks. I roll my eyes.

"Yeah, you could say that," I mutter.

"Shacking up with a teacher in the first week? Classy, Mackenzie, really classy," a familiar, irritating voice says loudly from behind me. *How the fuck does Stella know where I am staying?*

"Hi, Stella," I say sweetly, turning to face her. "Want to practice for pain class?" She visibly pales at my comment, taking a slight step back.

"I'll pass on that, you little psycho. But, I guess you could always practice with Mr. Daniels? I hear pain can be very fun to play with in the bedroom," she comments. East chokes on his drink, and Logan thumps him on the back.

"You're staying with Mr. Daniels?" he asks me directly, ignoring Stella.

"Yes, in the spare room. For safety," I reply blankly. Stella laughs, a harsh, forced sound.

"For safety? That's the excuse you're going with? Cute," she says, deliberately speaking loud enough so that the people at the surrounding tables can hear. By lunch, everyone will know where I'm staying. And, they will be assuming it's for completely different reasons than the true one. *Great.*

"Yes, for safety. Rogues attacked the Academy last night if you didn't notice," I say sarcastically.

"And, you're getting special treatment because?" she snaps.

"Because she's got twelve marks and is a target, obviously. Get a fucking grip and get lost, Stella," Enzo's voice floats over. Stella steps to the side and reveals Enzo standing there, holding two trays. He takes a seat at the table, sliding one breakfast-filled tray across to me, and the other in front of himself.

"Hey, Enzo. I didn't see you there," Stella practically purrs, completely ignoring the fact he plainly just told her to take a hike.

"Stella, go crawl back into whatever cave you came out of," Locke mutters.

"Fuck off, Logan," she spits back.

I laugh. "That's Locke," I chirp.

"Does it fucking matter? They're basically just one annoying person anyway," Stella says, earning glares from all of us. "Fine, I'm going. The standards over at this table have clearly dropped too low for me to stick around anyway," she says, looking pointedly at me and Kelly. Relief washes over me as she walks away. I was moments from slapping the sense into her.

"You're staying with Mr. Daniels?" East asks again quietly, repeating his earlier question.

"Yes, for safety," I say, repeating my previous answer. "Is there a problem with that?" He stares silently at me, considering for a while before shrugging.

"I guess not," he says casually, but I can see the intense looks he is giving the twins. I decide to ignore it.

"Thanks for breakfast," I mumble to Enzo.

"I was only trying to save my own. I could see you stealing Logan's from over there, and decided you having your own would be my best chance at keeping my food to myself," he answers coldly.

"Sure. Thanks anyway," I say, trying to stop the smug smile creeping over my face. *He's not a complete ass then.*

"What classes have you got today, Kenz?" Kelly asks, moving the conversation onto a lighter tone.

"Um, Transmutation, and the app said it's an all-day class for the first one," I answer. "You've got electives today, right?"

"Yup, marked history and literature. The history teacher is apparently a total bore though, so I am already regretting that decision," she replies.

"You can drop it if it's crap though, right?" I ask, taking a bite of bacon. *Gods that's good.*

"Yes, only after the end of term, though," she says sighing.

"You'll probably die of boredom by then," Locke says, tapping his fingers on the table, having already finished his food.

"That bad?" I ask.

"Even he falls asleep teaching that class," Logan answers, a smirk crossing his face.

"Have fun," I tease Kelly. A frown crosses her face.

"I think I may regret taking so many electives," she says softly.

"Most definitely, the best part about having less powers is all the free time. I'm kind of jealous," Locke says. She bites her lip, clearly holding something back. Instead, she just smiles and nods politely. *Damn, she really is still worked up about having two marks.*

"Better to be a master of two marks than a master of none," I chime. She rolls her eyes.

"But, it's better to be a master of all twelve," she teases.

"I'll be lucky if I can cover the basics in each," I reply. "Just too much effort to become a master. I'd rather watch Netflix."

"You're such a bad liar," she replies.

"You should probably do more eating and less talking, Kenz. We've gotta be in transmutation in fifteen minutes," Easton says, interrupting us.

"Fine, fine," I mutter, shovelling more food in my mouth. Far too much food at once. I can feel my cheeks are slightly puffed out. I grin at him, he just shakes his head smiling at me, before going back to finishing his own food. We finish off our food, and I walk out with East, keeping my eyes on the floor and away from everyone in the room who I know are staring.

"So, who teaches transmutation?" I ask East as we make our way outside the academy and towards the woods, where the class is apparently being held. It's freezing out here, and I pull my coat closer around me. *Why are all the classes outside when there are buildings with heating?*

"Mr. Daniels," East says, his voice dripping with annoyance. I glance at East as he moves slightly closer to me, and his arm brushes mine. We haven't had a chance to talk since the kiss yesterday and everything that happened after. I want to talk to him about it, but know it's not the best idea right now. I haven't even had a chance to tell Kelly about what happened. She's never going to believe sexy East kissed me.

"Don't you like him?" I ask.

"I respect him, but I don't trust him around you, Kenz," East says just as we come into the clearing, and a group of students are standing in a circle, with Mr. Daniels in the middle. His eyes meet mine, and he waves us over. Mr. Daniels looks good today in a black coat, his soft-brown hair is brushed to one side, and he is freshly shaven. I can't look away as we stop in the gap in the circle, and Mr. Daniels gives me a strange look, his eyes drifting to East before looking away.

"Now that everyone is here, we can start. I'm Mr. Daniels, and this is your first transmutation class.

CECE ROSE AND G. BAILEY

Transmutation is the ability to shift into an animal, and it's a powerful mark to have. Now, animals are individual to each person. There's no way to know what you will get until you try."

"I heard that you are more likely to get the animals your parents have," a girl says, blushing when Mr. Daniels turns to look at her. A slight bit of jealousy flitters through me when he nods and replies to her.

"Yes, Annabelle. Sometimes animals run in the family, but that's not always the case. My parents both have the transmutation mark, and my wolf is different from theirs. They have a snake and rat," he tells her. She giggles and smiles at him. *Why does he know her first name?* I swallow down the bitter jealously I feel, deciding I just don't like the girl and keep listening as Mr. Daniels carries on talking.

"Some animals, like bears for example, are great for combat and others, like mice, are good for escaping. Either way, this class will teach you how to shift safely and still be in control. No matter the size of your animal, losing control and letting their instinct take over is easy. It's much harder to remember that you're human and not animal. That's something to think on when you shift, try to remember who you are. One more thing before we start. The first shift is difficult, painful even," he tells us and pauses as people start whispering. He flat out avoids looking at me as he carries on speaking. "So, we will take shifting one by one, and I will command you to shift back for the first time. I assume everyone read the message and understands about the protection mark?" he asks, everyone says yes, and I try to think back to what my dad said about the protection mark and shifting. I can't remember, and I'm sure it can't be that important anyway. "Those of you who do not have the protection mark will go last, we have a separate practice in place for you. Easton, Jacob, Skye, and Marcel, you are the only ones without protection here, correct?" he asks.

"I don't either, sir," another guy says. Mr. Daniels nods.

"Mr. Dawn please step forward," Mr. Daniels asks, and another guy with bright-ginger hair and a spotty face steps forward. "Please call your mark," Mr. Daniels suggests, and we all go quiet as we watch him shift. It takes a few minutes, but his body starts to glimmer. When the glimmering stops, there's a small ginger cat sitting on the ground. The cat shakily takes a step forward and then stops, looking up at Mr. Daniels before rolling on the floor and showing his belly. I wouldn't be able to tell that's anything other than a normal cat at one glance. I wonder how many marked shift into normal animals and just walk around?

"Shift," Mr. Daniels says with such power in his voice that it makes me want to cower from him. His voice is deep, dark almost, and reminds me just how powerful he is. I have a feeling that Mr. Daniels is constantly holding back with his power, and could do much more than most. The cat glimmers once more, and the guy is back, kneeling and he shakes a little as he stands.

"Brilliant first shift. Well done, Mr. Dawn," Mr.

Daniels says and claps. We clap, too as the guy blushes and takes a step back. Two more people shift while we wait, one into a large horse and another into a lion. Mr. Daniels congratulates them both, and I whisper to East,

"What do you shift into?"

"A hawk," he whispers back, moving closer and placing his hand on the middle of my back. That must be a sight to see, and it kind of suits him.

"Miss Crowe, if you would leave your boyfriend for a second and come here? I have called you twice," Mr. Daniels says, and there's an awkward silence as I look back at him. He isn't looking at me, no, he is glaring at East. *What is his problem?*

"Sure," I say stepping forward.

"Please call your mark, Miss Crowe," he tells me as I stop in the middle of the circle. I call the mark into my mind, imagining the circle with dozens of lines in the middle of it and they all cross over. The first thing I feel is a slight pain in my hip where the mark is, and then it spreads, causing me to close my eyes and hold in the urge to scream. The pain washes over my body like a wave, feeling like it hits every part of me before it stops. I blink open my eyes, feeling how different my body feels straight away. I stretch slightly, seeing large paws instead of arms in front of me and somehow it doesn't freak me out. My fur is white and everything seems a little more in focus than I've ever seen it. I can see the white flecks of dust in the air, and when I take a deep breath, the strong smells of the people around me. I look up, as a deep voice speaks,

"Shift, Miss Crowe," I hear, and I shake my head, knocking off the urge to do as he said. I don't want to. I go to tell him no, and a loud growl comes out, instead. I must be a wolf or a dog. I look over at Mr. Daniels, seeing that I'm about half the size of him, so a large animal definitely.

"Come back, Mackenzie," another voice says next to me as I hear steps on the grass and look up into East's worried face as he crouches down a few steps away from me. *East, I remember East.*

"Shift," the deep voice says again, and all I hear is the demand, the challenge in his deep voice. I turn to look at Mr. Daniels, and no part of me stops as I jump at him. He catches me mid-air as I snap my teeth at him, wanting to challenge him back. We land on the floor with a smack, and I hear him groan in pain, my teeth inches away from his neck. The jolt shocks me out of whatever that was, and I remember who he is, who I am. I push the mark away in my mind, begging for my normal body back. When a slight bite of pain starts at my hip and spreads across my body, I welcome it and close my eyes. When I start to feel normal again, I smile down at Mr. Daniels and see a paw turn into a hand on his shoulder. My hair falls down my body, my very naked body. *Shit.*

"Kenz . . .," East's horrified voice comes from behind me, and the chilly air hits my back. *I'm naked on top of Mr. Daniels.*

"Everyone look away before I make you," East threatens as I try to keep very still on top of Mr. Daniels as I feel every part of him against me. *Gods, this is not how I wanted to get naked with Mr. Daniels, not one little bit.*

"Get her a jacket, now," Mr. Daniels says as I stand up, and he keeps his eyes off my body. I try to cover myself up as East comes over, shirtless, and hands me his shirt. I slip it over my head, and it, thankfully, falls to my knees. I pull my hair out of the shirt and look over at the shredded pile of clothes where I must have shifted. Thankfully my phone and shoes seem to have made it, but nothing else. I walk over and slip them on, picking up my phone and looking back at Mr. Daniels who runs his hands over his face.

"Go back to your room, Miss Crowe. We will speak about how to use the protection mark to keep your clothes on later. Easton, go with her," Mr. Daniels tells him, and I'm shocked enough to glance at East who shakes his head at me. *Shit, that's what the protection ward was for.* Now that I think about it, I remember seeing a note on my phone last night about reading up on the protection ward for the class. *Whoops.*

"The rest of you, get back into the circle. Please remember to use the protection ward," he says, and I hear a few snickers around me. *Great.* It won't be long until this gets around the school, too, I bet. I walk away towards Mr. Daniels cabin, which is thankfully not far. *I wonder if any of my classes are going to go normally?*

Chapter 21
KENZIE

"*H*ere, the key is under the pot. Mr. Daniels showed me it last night," I say when East tries to open the door to Mr. Daniels' cabin. The cabin is far outside the school, practically in the middle of the woods and a far distance from the other teacher's cabins. *I wonder why he wanted to be so alone out here?* I pick the plant pot up and pull the key out, handing it to East who opens the door to the cabin.

I walk in after East, admiring how nice Mr. Daniels' cabin is on the inside. It has a modern leather sofa and a large fireplace with a big TV above it. There is a big, fur rug in front of the fire, which is thick and looks real. I didn't get a chance to look around much last night, so I walk over to the picture frames on the fireplace. There is a picture of a young girl who looks about eight in the picture. She looks so familiar, with her brown hair and green eyes, but I can't place where I've seen her before. There's another picture of an old couple, that are clearly his parents as the man in the picture looks just like Mr. Daniels. I quickly glance around the rest of the room, not seeing many other personal effects. There is a small pile of books on the window ledge, but that's it.

"He has a nice place," East comments, and I look over to see him walk into the small kitchen. There are five rooms: two bedrooms, the lounge, the kitchen and a large bathroom. It's cosy and strange to think I'm going to be living here with Mr. Daniels for the rest of the year. My attraction to him is only getting worse, and being around him all the time is going to be a nightmare.

"I'm going to get dressed," I tell East, gesturing down at my body dressed only in his shirt. I turn to go to the guest room when he grabs my arm and stops me. I pause and look up at him quizzically.

"Kenz," he whispers, staring back down at me. I feel heat rush through me from the intensity of his gaze. I'm not able to shift my mind from our kiss yesterday, or the fact he saw me completely naked just minutes ago. *I wonder if he liked what he saw? Fuck.*

"What?" I manage to mumble back, taking note of the fact he looks so much better minus his shirt. *Maybe I'll just keep it? I'd be doing the world a public service. Shirtless Easton Black, thank me later, world.*

"You didn't do that on purpose, did you?" he asks gently, but I feel like I've been slapped, or had a bucket of ice thrown over me. *He couldn't be serious?*

"What? I just embarrassed myself in front of our entire class! Why the hell would you think I did that on purpose?" He flinches from the bite in my words, pulling back.

"I don't know, Kenz. Maybe to get Mr. Daniels' attention?" he says, not looking me in the eyes anymore.

"You think I need to throw myself naked at someone to get their attention?" I ask him incredulously.

"No. Shit, Kenz, you're taking this all wrong," he mutters, running a hand through his hair.

"I'm taking this wrong? You're accusing me of jumping naked onto our teacher for attention, or what, to seduce him? You think I'm trying to sleep with my teacher?" I question him, narrowing my eyes. He looks back at me silently, his eyes telling me all I need to know.

"You know what, East, get out," I say, gesturing at the door.

"Kenz, wait. I think—"

"I said, get out!" I shout, losing my temper. I feel my marks start to respond to my emotional distress without my calling them. The room shakes and several objects are hovering above their rightful places.

"Kenzie, just breathe a minute," he says softly, stepping towards me slowly, as if approaching a skittish animal. "You need to calm down." *He really didn't just say that, right?*

"And, you need to leave. You know what, maybe I do want to take my clothes off with Mr. Daniels, but

I'm not really sure if that's any of your business," I snap. His head snaps up, and he looks me right in the eyes. I don't look away from him as he stares at me, but I hear things breaking around the room and the ground starts lightly shaking.

"Fine, I'm going." *Shit. Maybe I went too far?* He walks to the door and then pauses, turning back to face me. "I'm gonna need my shirt, but I can wait a minute," he says, leaning against the door. Without hesitation, I pull his shirt off over my head and throw it at him. Standing completely naked as I glare in his direction. He gapes at me, holding the shirt in his hands. *Well, he said he wanted his shirt back.*

"You can go now. Don't forget to shut the door behind you," I say, turning around and storming into the guest room, slamming the door behind me.

I lean my back against it, breathing in and out deeply, trying to calm myself down. I hear the main door to the cabin slam shut and cringe from the harsh sound of it. He left. *Well what do you expect, dumbass? You told him to go.* I put my head in my hands and groan, rubbing at my temples. *Why do I have to go and open my mouth like that?*

After a while, my breathing returns to normal, and I feel my powers retreat. Thank gods for that. I move from the door and rummage through my bags for clothes, having not unpacked yet from moving in here. I pull out a red lace matching set of underwear and pull it on quickly. I hear the front door open and close again. *Fucking East.*

I turn around and shove open the guest room door, storming out into the main living area.

"East, I thought I told you to—" my words cut off as I spot who has actually entered into the cabin.

"Kenzie, I would have thought you would have had time to put clothes on by now," Enzo teases, not looking away. I roll my eyes. I can't even be bothered to be embarrassed anymore. My whole class, my hot teacher, and Easton have already seen me butt naked today. *What's a little walking around in my underwear going to hurt now?*

"I thought you were East," I mutter, walking over to the open-planned kitchen area to grab a drink. Maybe Mr. Daniels has something a little stronger in here somewhere?

"Do you always greet East in your underwear?" he asks.

"Funny. What are you even doing here anyway, Enzo?" I ask, checking the fridge first.

"I was sent here to keep an eye on you. Mr. Daniels still has a class to teach, and they don't want you wandering around alone," he says and shrugs.

"So, they sent another student to watch me?" I ask dubiously.

"Not just any student, their best student," he replies, following me into the kitchen area. He hops onto the counter, taking a seat there as I continue to search. I huff.

"Sure, not even a tiny bit egotistical there at all, are you?" I ask, rolling my eyes.

"I'm not, it's a fact. I could have already finished

and left this place if I wanted to, as it is I'm set to finish this year, instead of next," he replies, not an ounce of exaggeration in his voice.

"Whatever," I mutter as I open the last cupboard and spot a glass bottle hiding in the back. *Bingo.* I pull out the bottle of Vodka and place it on the kitchen side, and go in search of glasses. *I'm sure I just saw them.*

"What are you doing?" Enzo questions.

"What does it look like, Mr. Know-It-All?" I question back sarcastically as I place a couple of frosted, coloured glasses on the kitchen side. "How do you want it?"

"Straight, I guess," he mutters. I roll my eyes, typical macho attitude. I pour some vodka into each glass, and top mine up with some Pepsi from the fridge. I hand a glass to him, he takes it, clinking it against mine.

"Cheers," I mutter.

"What are we drinking to?" he asks, amusement colouring his tone.

"Embarrassment," I reply wryly, before downing half my drink in one go. He drinks some of his. I lift mine back up and finish it off, going to pour myself another.

"Slow down," he comments, knocking back some more of his own.

"What, worried you can't keep up?" I tease. I down another drink, then I grab the vodka, Pepsi, and my glass and head into the main living room area. I sink down onto the leather sofa, feeling the cool material clinging against my bare skin. I can already feel a light buzz hitting me. Enzo takes the spot next to me, sitting much closer than he really needs to, his eyes running over me constantly.

Two can play at that game, buddy. I turn in my spot on the sofa, stretching my bare legs out across his. I take a swig straight from the bottle, trying not show the burn I feel on my throat as it makes its way down. I hand the bottle to Enzo, who silently takes a swig too, before handing it back.

"You wanna talk about it?" he asks.

"Not really," I mutter.

"What do you wanna do then?" he asks, the slight curve to his sensual lips giving me all kinds of bad ideas. *I wonder what kind of ideas are going through his head?*

"I don't know," I answer, before taking another swig. The burn is slightly less noticeable this time, which can only mean one thing.

"I think you know," he replies, looking down at me. His dark eyes are staring at me intently. *He's really putting in no effort to hide his visual pursuit of my body.* Well, if he's going to keep staring, I might as well have some fun with this, tease him a little.

"What do you think I want?" I ask seductively. I move over him, sliding a leg on either side of him, so I'm straddling his lap. He visibly swallows. I can feel his body responding to me. Or, maybe he's been like that since he walked in and found me half naked?

"Kenzie," he breathes.

"What?" I whisper, running a hand down the front of his body absently. Feeling his toned body, I almost forget my plan. He groans as I reach the top of his jeans. I brush my fingers lightly over the edge of the waistband. Leaning down against him, I put my lips to his ear, brushing them against his earlobe lightly. "Stop staring, it's not gonna happen," I whisper. I pull back slightly and meet his eyes. I'm sure smugness is painted across my face, as realisation crosses his. He narrows his dark eyes on me and opens his mouth to say something, when the door opens. It lets a gust of chilly air into the cabin, I feel it hit my skin, as well as the gaze of the person who opened the door.

"What the fuck is going on in here, Enzo, Miss Crowe?" Mr. Daniels' voice calls into the cabin. He eyes take in the bottle of vodka on the floor next to the sofa, the two glasses on the table in front of us, and me. Sitting half naked on Enzo's lap. *Great, just damn, fucking peachy.*

"I can explain," I say, turning slightly to face him, feeling the heat rise into my cheeks. Enzo leans back and begins laughing. "Shut up," I mutter. I slide off him and stand up, wrapping my arms around my body self-consciously. *Is he really going to make me stand here half-naked and explain? Or can I go grab some clothes first?*

"Well?" he asks, crossing his arms and raising an eyebrow.

"Um, well . . .," I trail off, trying to think of some kind of explanation for what he walked in on. *'I'm sorry, sir, I just figured after embarrassing myself in front of the whole class by getting naked and jumping on you, followed by arguing with Easton, that getting drunk with Enzo in my underwear was a great idea.'* It sounds terrible even to me.

"I'm waiting," he drawls. "Enzo, what about you, any explanation?"

"You don't hide your booze well enough?" he mutters, but I'm standing close enough to catch it.

"I'm sorry, what was that?" Mr. Daniels asks.

"Nothing, sir. Just remarking how chilly Kenzie must be with you leaving the door open. Maybe she should go finish getting dressed?" Enzo asks. A wash of gratitude hits me. I really don't deserve him being nice after that. Turning back, I shoot him a grateful smile before looking again at Mr. Daniels, who is staring at me, deciding what to do. *Or, maybe he's —* *Nope, not today, Satan.* I shut that thought up before it can finish forming.

"Fine, Miss Crowe, please go finish getting dressed. We can talk about this in a minute. Enzo, please come outside with me for a moment?" he finally says. Letting out a breath, I turn and make my way into the guest room. I catch Enzo's eyes as I'm closing the door, but I'm not able to read the look in them.

Just what is he thinking?

Chapter 22

ENZO

"Go on then." I wave a hand at Mr. Daniels as he stops outside the cabin and slams the door shut, resting his head against it. I know I'm going to get a lecture on behaviour or whatever else he has planned. I look over at him, wanting to know how angry he is, but the defeated look he is wearing confuses me. There's a long, uncomfortable silence, and I look back through the cabin window, catching a glance of Kenzie as she walks towards the bedroom, the lacy red underwear turning me on.

She is something else, and I don't think I've ever liked a girl as much as I like her. I remember the first time I saw her, walking down the middle of the hall with determined eyes and wet hair. She was beautiful, but that wasn't the only thing I liked. She didn't care what anyone said, what anyone thought about her.

"Miss Crowe doesn't need these kinds of distractions," Mr. Daniels starts off, and I just smirk at him as I lean against the cabin. When I got the message in class from the teacher that Mr. Daniels needed me to watch Kenzie, I was curious why he sent me. I doubt he knew how close I was getting to Kenzie, and I saw East stomping through the woods away from the cabin. I think he didn't trust East around her alone.

"You might as well call her Kenzie. We both know you're bullshitting me that she is just a student to you," I say, knowing that he won't lie to me. I've been friends with him since we were kids. Our parents lived near each other, and he was the big kid I looked up to and followed around. Eventually, he got bored of me annoying him and took me under his wing. I know him too well, and the look he gave Kenzie in there was a look I've seen plenty of times with his past girlfriends.

"While I'm here, she is my student," he tells me, confirming my thoughts that he likes her. *I wonder if Kenzie realises how much?*

"Why are you here?" I ask him, and he shrugs, looking away. It doesn't make any sense. When he finished the academy two years ago, he was the highest ranking marked in years. It didn't surprise me, as I know how powerful he is with his eight marks. It was a surprise when I got more marks than him, and he helped me master them all quickly, the ones he could, anyway. But, I know he passed everything with flying colours and was given a job with the council.

Everyone, including me, knew he would get a place on the council. Even with the issues with his sister—how he let her go, and now she is with the rogues. I grew up with her around, too, and never guessed how she felt about the rebels, how she wanted to be one.

"To watch Kenzie. I was sent here to guard her, the council sent me. She is too important," he says, and I nod, looking back into the empty room. It makes a lot of sense, considering no one knows what the twelfth power is, or if it's controllable at all. I bet the council want to make sure Kenzie can be controlled, and the best way to do that, is to send a young, powerful, and good-looking teacher to stalk her. I can't help but wonder if they want them to get *close?* An easy way to have more control of her.

"Can you guard her? Without being jealous?" I ask him, and he narrows his eyes at me.

"I'm not jealous of anyone," he says bluntly, and I just laugh quietly, watching as he gets more annoyed.

"We can both have her . . . just a thought," I tell him as I walk down the cabin steps and into the woods. I don't expect him to reply to me, but he does. His voice is quiet, but I still catch it.

"Not yet."

Just two words that speak a lot more than they should, but I understand the meaning behind them anyway.

Not turning to look at him, I walk away into the woods and follow the path back to the school. I pull the back door of the school open, waiting for two girls to walk through and then close it behind me. I walk up the stairs to my room, needing to find my phone and then get to my elective class. I open my room, surprised to see East and Logan in there. They are playing Xbox and talking quietly. The room looks like a tip on one side, clothes everywhere, and I like mine neat. I pick up a few of Logan's shirts as I walk past and chuck them into the washing basket by the door. *Thank gods for the cleaners and their insistence on washing all our clothes every night.* They are always back, neatly folded in the morning.

"Don't you have class?" Logan asks, and I shake my head.

"I had to stay with Kenzie until Mr. Daniels came back," I say, deciding not to explain that I had her half naked on my lap, and she knows how much she turned me on. It took everything in me not to kiss her and fuck her on Mr. Daniels' couch. Now, that would have made him mad, had I slept with Kenzie before he can even make a move. East turns to look at me, looking stressed.

"I fucked it up with her, was she still mad?" he asks. *So that's why she was like that, East pissed her off. It makes some sense.*

"If you call walking around in just your underwear and getting drunk on vodka mad, then yeah," I answer, and he groans, running his hand through his hair.

"I thought . . . well, I thought she might have shifted back naked in front of Mr. Daniels on purpose. I've seen plenty of girls do it before her, but they didn't jump on him first," he says. *What an idiot.*

"You did what?" Logan asks, before whacking him on the arm.

"Fuck, that hurt, and yeah, I know. I'm surprised she didn't do more than just throw me out. I regretted my words the minute I said them," East says, both his voice and face turning glum.

"Kenzie isn't like the rest of the girls. I don't know her well and didn't grow up with her like you did, but I know she wouldn't do that. She isn't like that," I tell him. I know because she didn't kiss me or throw herself at me like every girl usually does. It gets boring after a while, and Kenzie is anything but boring, and East seems to realise this. He has as many girls throwing themselves at him as I do in this damn place. Being that there are more guys born than girls, seems to make the girls here think they can fuck any guy and that guy is lucky to have them. Which isn't true, but most of the girls around here have personalities like pampered princesses.

"Fuck. I should go and say sorry or something," East says, turning off the Xbox and putting the controller down.

"You're gonna have to do more than that. You need a big gesture," Logan says, and East shrugs.

"Like what?" East replies as I sit down on the bed.

"Something big and romantic. Like in the human movies," Logan suggests.

I sit and listen to their insane plan and don't make any suggestions. Kenzie can tease me all she likes, but this will be amusing to watch as a comeback. The best part is, it isn't even me doing it.

Chapter 23

KENZIE

"Would you like pasta for dinner? I can make you some," Mr. Daniels says gently as I come into the kitchen a few moments after getting dressed in jeans and a thick, long-sleeved, jumper. I tried to choose something that covered me the most, feeling that I've been naked enough today. I still feel a little drunk, but the whole getting caught by your teacher, half naked on a couch with a hot guy, has a way of sobering you up. I nod, confused why he isn't shouting at me and watch as he moves around the kitchen, pulling out pans and food. I expected a massive lecture about underage drinking and what it looked like I was doing with Enzo on his couch. I mean, he invited me into his home, and I do that on the next day. I feel like such a bitch and seriously guilty over it.

"Can I help?" I ask him and he looks over his

shoulder for a second, his eyes meeting mine and then turning back.

"You could grate the cheese," he offers, pointing a finger towards a plate and grater he has gotten out. I pick them up and get the cheese out of the fridge before starting to grate the cheese like he asked.

There's an uncomfortable silence between us that just seems to go on and on before I cave in and blurt out: "I'm sorry for today, all of it. I know you must think I'm an irresponsible brat or something, but I swear it won't happen again. I just seem to have a habit of messing things up, and I get it if you don't want to speak to me,"

"What happened today made me realise something," he starts to say and then clears his throat, putting down the pasta packet he was opening. Mr. Daniels walks over to me, resting his hip on the counter and crossing his arms. He stares at me for a long time, before uncrossing his arms and tucking a bit of hair behind my ear, his fingers grazing across my cheek.

"Yes?" I ask, my voice a little bit too high-pitched. He goes to say something when the door is banged on a few times, and he closes his mouth, annoyance written all over his face.

"I'll get it," I say, moving away and feeling his eyes burning a hole through my back as I walk to the door. I pull it open, and Kelly is standing there, smiling widely. She looks lovely, in a white coat and her blonde hair up in some complicated bun. I've really got to ask her to do to my hair at some point.

"So, naked Kenzie, I think we need to talk," she says, and I laugh. So, she heard, which means everyone must be talking about it. *Great, just fucking great.*

"Come on in," I say, holding the door open. She walks in and looks around for a second, just before Mr. Daniels walks over.

"Kelly, right?" he asks, holding out a hand, and she shakes it.

"Yes. I just came to say hello to Kenzie and catch up," she says.

"Sure, why don't you show her your room, and I'll keep cooking. Kelly, would you like some pasta for dinner?" he asks, and she nods.

"Are you sure you don't need any help?" I ask him, still wondering what he was going to say to me earlier.

"No," he says, moving away and back to the kitchen. I hook my arm in Kelly's and walk us down towards my room, pushing the door open. The room is simple, with blue sheets on a single bed and matching, dark-blue curtains. There's another fur rug in here and a wardrobe with a matching chest of drawers. I still need to get some more of my things from my old room, but I managed to get most of it in here. Kelly goes in and sits on the bed, as I shut the door.

"So . . .?" she asks, raising her eyebrows as she trails off. I don't know where to start. So much has happened in the last twenty-four hours, and I haven't a clue how to explain it all.

"Sexy East kissed me, then saw me naked in the bath. Then the twins also saw me naked in the bath.

Then, I shifted back naked on top of Mr. Daniels and in front of the whole class. And then, East was a dick to me, despite the fact he has seen me naked twice now. Then, Enzo and I got drunk, like vodka from the bottle drunk."

"There's a whole lot of naked in that statement," Kelly says, her eyes widening, and it makes me laugh.

"Yeah. I don't think I've been naked this much since I was a baby," I reply.

"So naked on top of Mr. Daniels, was that fun?" she asks jokingly, waggling her eyebrows.

"Totally, the whole class staring and laughing at me really set the mood," I answer.

"Do you think it's going to make this awkward, you staying here with him?" she asks, her voice turning more serious.

"It's beyond awkward, but hey, maybe I'll catch him naked sometime," I joke.

"If you do, do the world a favour and commit the view to perfect memory . . . and then recount it for me. I'm living my relationship life vicariously through you. I'm relying on you here," she teases.

"I don't know why," I mutter.

"There's just nobody here for me," she says and sighs dramatically, lying back on my bed.

"Come off it, Kells. You know there are plenty of guys in the academy who would be interested in you," I reply, sitting on the edge of the bed with my back against the wall.

"Not the right ones," she mumbles, throwing an arm over her eyes.

"What's that supposed to mean? You have a particular guy in mind?" I ask.

"No, what would make you think that?" she asks, a little too quickly.

"Kelly Curwood, you vixen. Who is this man, and why haven't I been told all the details?" I ask her.

"Nobody," she says, again too quickly.

"Oh my god, I know it, right? I must, if you won't tell me," I say.

"There's nobody, you're being ridiculous," Kelly replies.

"Sure, What's Mr. Nobody's name, Kells?" I ask her.

"There's really no—"

"I will tickle the information out of you," I say seriously, cutting her off. She moves her hand from over her face and looks me dead in the eye.

"You wouldn't," she says.

"Try me," I reply sweetly.

"Fine," she says and then sighs. "There is someone."

"I knew it!" I exclaim.

"But, it's complicated. He wouldn't want me now, anyway," she says, her voice sounding defeated.

"Why wouldn't he?" I ask.

"Because I have two marks, just two. He's got way more and is way too good for me," she mutters.

"The amount of marks you have doesn't matter, Kells," I say to her softly, squishing in to lie beside her.

"We kissed once, me and the guy," she says, it comes across wistful.

"When was that?" I ask curiously, dying to get some more information out of her. It's not like Kelly to be so lock-lipped about this kind of thing.

"Months ago," she sighs. "It only happened once, and he didn't seem that interested after," she says.

"Wait, you've been crushing on mystery man for months and haven't told me?" I ask.

"Maybe . . .," she says trailing off as she looks away.

"Who is he?" I ask, feeling even more curious now. She goes to answer when a knock comes at the door.

"Dinner's ready," Mr. Daniels' voice calls through the door. Now that he mentions it, I can definitely smell the scent of the food slipping through the gaps in the door.

"You may be saved by my desire for food right now, but you are going to give me all the juicy information later, got it?" I say to Kelly.

"Fine," she grumbles, but she doesn't meet my eyes as she says it.

"But first, let's go eat lots of pasta," I reply lightly, letting her off the hook for now. I feel my stomach grumble in agreement as I stand. *At least, something is communicating properly with me.* I watch Kelly as she stands and heads toward the door. *She's hiding something more than just a name, and I intend to find out what.*

Chapter 24

KENZIE

"*W*elcome to earth class, Miss Crowe. Nice to see you're keeping with what I've heard from the other teachers," a small lady says as I approach her and the rest of the class, who are sitting on the ground in the middle of a clearing in the woods. *Did they really have to make all my classes so hard to find?*

I take a better look at the teacher. She's a small woman, no more than 5ft, with a tiny frame to match. Her hair is tied back in a neat, professional bun. and her clothing looks more like a secretary, than an earth power teacher.

"Sorry, Miss. I'm not sure what you mean?" I ask as I take a seat on the floor next to Logan. I smile at Logan, and he looks at me pityingly. *Crap, what now?*

"You're fifteen minutes late, Miss Crowe. It's nice to know that you are at least consistent. That being said, I do hope you don't intend to remove your clothes during this class, too," she says. A few snickers come from other students. I try to think of a retort when I feel Logan nudging me in the side. I turn and look at him, he shakes his head slightly. *Shutting up it is, I guess.*

"Sorry for being late," I mumble.

"I'm sure," she says sarcastically. "Now, seeing as you missed the beginning of my introduction, I'm wondering what you can tell me about the earth mark and what it can do. Or, will I need to repeat that information for you?" she asks me.

"The earth mark is one of the most versatile marks. It can be used both as a simple control over natural matter, like moving rocks. Or it can be used in stuff like helping plants grow or curing the rot from a tree," I answer. She stares at me for a moment as if surprised by my answer, before turning back to the class as a whole and continuing to lecture on the topic.

"How did you know that?" Logan whispers.

"One of my mum's most powerful marks is earth. You should see our garden," I answer quietly, before turning back to listen to the teacher.

"Now, class, I would first like to focus on the more nature-focused aspect of this mark." She grabs a black bag from the ground next to her, and pulls out some flowers, dead looking flowers. *No prizes for guessing what we were going to be doing today.* "Take one and hand the rest along, Lucinda," she says, passing them to the girl nearest to her. She does as she says, and the flowers pass along the two rows of seated students until we all have one. *Now we've all got a dead flower. Fantastic.*

"Now, I want you to place the stem of the flower to the ground. You will call on your mark, and try to reconnect your flower to the ground by growing its roots," she explains.

I lay my flower down onto the ground, keeping a hand on it as I picture the earth mark in my head. A leaf curled into a circle. It's one of the smaller marks, usually coming out a lot smaller on people's skin than the others.

Calling on the mark and placing my other hand on the ground next to the flower, I'm waiting for something to happen. When the roots don't immediately grow, and the flower doesn't spring back into life, I huff and sit back, glancing around at the rest of the class. They appear to be having more success than I am. Some of them have already got the roots grown back, whereas others have completed the exercise and have pretty, live looking flowers in front of them. I put my hands back on the flower, covering where the stem meets the ground. *Maybe if I can't actually see it, it'll work better.*

I call on the mark again, feeling it respond to my call this time. I push as much energy into the plant as I can all at once, not wanting to be the last to finish the task we have been given.

A bird cries overhead, and I look up, making sure it's not flying over me. *It would just be my luck if it shit on my head. I try and spot the bird, but can't see it anywhere.*

"Kenzie?" Logan says, dragging my attention to him. I turn to face him.

"What?" I ask.

"What are you doing? The ground . . .," he trails off.

I look down at the ground, lifting my hands away. My flower has grown roots and come to life, but all the grass within ten feet of me has grown too. Thick, lush, and deep-green, nothing like the state it was in just moments before. I notice the grass is still growing, flowers shooting out from the ground, the effect spreading even further. The whole class has turned to face me, the direct centre of the circle of green. I release the hold on the mark in my mind, stopping the flow of magic.

"Well, there is no need to show off, Mackenzie," the teacher says, but she's smiling now. *Maybe I'm forgiven for being late?*

"Shit, Kenzie. Were you even trying?" Logan whispers.

"Kind of? I was trying to do it quickly, so I pushed more energy into it, I'm not sure how the rest of this happened . . .," I trail off, looking at the thick sea of green around me.

"Energy has to go somewhere, I guess. The flower didn't need anymore, so the excess energy spread and gave life to everything else," he supplies.

"That would be correct, Logan," the teacher cuts in, having made her way across to us so quietly I hadn't noticed her approach. "You will have to be careful with your gift, Mackenzie. Although it is good that the earth responds so easily to you, things are meant to die. We respect nature's cycle, for the most part. Just giving it helping hands along the way. So, don't go bringing every dull field to life now," she jokes.

"I won't," I answer anyway.

"Good," she replies to me, she then directs her attention to the whole class again. "We will now focus on what is normally the showier aspect of the earth power, manipulation." She goes back to her black bag and pulls out some smooth, black stones, handing one to each of us. "Place the stone on the ground in front of you," she instructs. I place mine on the ground next to Logan's.

"This is just like moving rocks, right?" I ask Logan softly.

"Pretty much, but some people can bring a whole house down, and some can cause large-scale earthquakes," he replies. I nod my head, having heard about a huge castle once brought to ruins by an earth marked's power.

"All I want you to do for now, class, is to bring the stone into your hand. For those of you with the air marks, no cheating and using the air to bring it to you," she explains. Everyone affirms their agreement with mumbles. "Oh and, Mackenzie?" she asks.

"Yes, Miss?"

"Try not to cause an earthquake," she replies dryly.

"I make no promises," I quip, holding my hand out towards my rock. This time I try not to focus on what everyone else is doing, and concentrate my focus solely onto my rock. I try to make it roll to me, calling on my earth mark, as I'm picturing that curved leaf in my head. Nothing. It doesn't even twitch. Cautiously, I push more power into my call. I wait for a moment, expecting something to happen but nothing. I try pushing more energy into it, slowly at first, but then just shoving as much into the damn rock as I can. I can feel sweat beading on my forehead. No matter how much I push into it, nothing happens. Not a damn thing.

"Are you okay, Kenzie?" Logan asks.

"It's not working," I reply, releasing the pull on my power.

"Sometimes people can only use one side of the earth power," he explains softly.

"I know that, but I guess I didn't think I'd be one of them," I reply. He brushes a strand of hair from my face and tucks it behind my ear.

"You don't have to be good at everything," he says.

"I guess," I reply, feeling a little bummed. *No earthquakes for me, I suppose.*

"Hey, don't look so glum. You might still be able to, maybe you just need to practice?"

"I know, it's just everything else has kind of come pretty easily."

"Maybe you have to struggle with the rest of us mere mortals now?" he teases. I roll my eyes. And then, I find myself looking at him, noticing how his shirt clings tightly against his broad frame. *With a body like his, he looks anything but a mere mortal.*

"What are you thinking?" he asks me.

"Nothing," I snap. "Why do you ask?"

"Because your eyes seemed to glaze over. It was the same look Locke gets when there's food," he teases.

"It was so not," I mutter.

"So, you're not hungry?" he asks, leaning back and incidentally giving me an even more impressive view as his arms tense from leaning back on them.

"A little," I admit. *But, it's not for food.*

He smiles a little knowingly at me before turning his gaze forward again, I let out a deep breath and do the same.

Chapter 25

KENZIE

"*A*re you going to talk to me?" East asks me for the fourth time since I walked into air class. I'm actually not late for once, but the teacher is. We have all been waiting for fifteen minutes now, and he or she is a no show. I try for the tenth time to turn my phone on, but it's not working. All I can see is my reflection across the cracked screen. My dark hair is all over the place, curly from the plait I had it in last night, and my pale eyes look tired.

"Kenz," East says my name softly, and I glance over at him as he leans across his desk. I want to forgive him, but I'm still so mad that I can't trust myself to respond to him at the moment. It really doesn't help that East looks amazing as usual today, with his wavy hair looking soft and his warm eyes watching me closely. *Why can't he look tired or less attractive and easier to ignore?* I just turn my head away and lean back in my chair, twirling my phone around on the table.

"Alright," East replies. Just when I think he is going to leave it and get that I don't want to speak to him, he stands on his desk and claps his hands. Everyone in the room looks at him as they go silent. We all watch on as he flips through his phone and then starts playing some music I don't recognise.

"I'm an idiot. The biggest idiot in the world. I said something really stupid and regretted it the moment I said it. So, I'm going to do anything, including begging or stripping, to get the lovely Kenzie to forgive me. I messed up and got the wrong impression when in reality, I was just jealous," he tells me and the entire class. Some part of me wants to see if he would actually strip in front of the whole class, but then he could get in a lot of trouble for this. I just raise an eyebrow, and he grins at me.

"I don't think you would strip, East," I laugh, feeling my cheeks going bright-red, and he grins down at me. East knows what he is doing to me, and most of me is embarrassed and another small part is impressed that he cares enough to do this.

"That sounded like a challenge, Kenzie," East says and slowly pulls his shirt off over his head and drops it on my table as some of the girls in the room stand up and move closer to watch. I don't take my eyes off East as I pick his shirt up and shake my head.

"Okay, okay, I get it. You're sorry," I laugh as he starts unbuttoning his jeans, and I can't help but stare at his naked chest. *Fucking hell, he looks amazing with no shirt on.* I'm half tempted not to give him his shirt back and actually let him strip out of all his clothes.

"I embarrassed you and fucked up yesterday, so I'm going to get naked in front of the whole class and give the school something else to talk about," he tells me quietly, making me wonder if he planned this, and if anyone else knew. They really should have stopped him. I'm a simple girl, I would have been happy with chocolate and a foot rub.

"East! I forgive you, you don't have to do that," I hiss as he starts pushing his jeans down slowly, in time to the music, and I laugh when I hear a girl shout over.

"Take it off!" she calls, and the whole class starts cheering. I can't blame them, East is one of the hottest guys in the academy. I'm sure most the girls in the school wouldn't have a problem with him stripping for them. East smirks down at me, just as his jeans fall to his ankles, showing off his tight, black boxers and the impressive package I can see. I pull my eyes away.

"What in the gods is going on in here?"

I look around East, seeing Mr. Layan standing in the doorway. The room goes instantly quiet, only the sound of the music still playing on East's phone making any sound. I lean over, turning the music off and handing East his phone back. Mr. Layan walks further into the room, and I can see that he has on a long, thick, black cloak, and his hood is down showing off his long, white hair and beady eyes. I try not to laugh at the disgusted look he is throwing everyone in the room as they go back to their seats.

"Put your shirt back on and get out of my class now," Mr. Layan snaps, and I hold in a smile when East laughs pulling his jeans up and jumps off the table.

"I'm the biggest idiot for many reasons, but give me another chance? Please, Kenz?" he asks me, ignoring everyone else in the room, and I sigh before nodding.

"Out," Mr. Layan shouts again as East takes his shirt from me and winks.

"I have to stay to watch Miss Crowe," East reminds Mr. Layan when he gets to the door, and I watch as they both stare at each other for a second. I can't see Mr Layan's expression, but he doesn't look happy.

"I am perfectly qualified to make sure Miss Crowe doesn't lose control of her gifts. Now, out and expect detention for the rest of the year," Mr. Layan says, and East nods, giving me a slightly worried look before walking out. It's strange to be without one of them around, but I know East couldn't have stayed in this class, and I'm sure I won't lose control of air. I couldn't even use it the other day.

"Your usual teacher isn't well, so you have me for your first class and maybe some others. I'm Mr. Layan, the headmaster of this academy, and I'm sure you have seen me around or heard of me," he says, his tone downright cocky, like he expects everyone to know exactly who he is and be in awe of him.

"I have ten marks, one of which is air. Can someone tell me something about the air mark?" he asks again in that cocky tone and there's silence around the room until a guy at the front puts his hand up and then starts speaking.

"Air is extremely difficult to use on its own, but works better with other element marked powers,"

"Very good, and yes, you are right. All elements can mix, some make others stronger and some can cancel each other out. Fire and air is destructive, and I wouldn't recommend mixing those for a while," Mr. Layan says and gives me a pointed look. *I'm never going to live that one down.*

"Water and air mix perfectly. Protection wards can stop extreme attacks from the air mark. Anyone care to tell me what happens when you mix earth and air?" he asks and everyone is silent, so I put a hand up and wait for him to nod before I answer.

"Tornados. Some of the biggest tornados around the world have been caused by marked using those powers wrong. My mother used to tell me that they shouldn't be used together at all unless you are certain you can control it."

"You are right, Miss Crowe. Now, open your textbooks and turn to page forty. I want you to read the next five chapters and write down the important notes." I pull the textbook on my desk towards me and find the page, only glancing up once before reading and seeing Mr. Layan watching me. A strange look crossing over his face.

"MISS CROWE, PLEASE WAIT," Mr. Layan says as I stand up at the end of class and put my phone in my pocket. *Gods, what now?* I pick my notes up off the table, folding the paper and sliding it into my coat pocket. The textbook is ridiculously boring and filled with useless information on the air mark. I can't see how I can use any of what I wrote down today. Mr. Layan just sat at the front of class, messing on his iPad. I bet he was playing a game by the way he was concentrating.

"Sure," I reply, walking towards him at the front of the classroom as everyone else leaves.

"I wish to show you something, come with me," he says, walking towards the door. I look away, groaning as I look out the window at the sun setting. I just want to get back to my room, steal Mr. Daniels' junk food, and collapse. Today has been a long day, and after this, it's going to be dark when I walk back through the woods.

"Come, Miss Crowe," Mr. Layan snaps as he holds the door open. I walk over and then follow him as he takes me down the busy corridors and towards the back of the academy. We walk into the empty hall, and he closes the doors behind us. The room is slowly getting dark, and I haven't been in here since I first got my marks. The twelve marks on the wall seem to glow almost from the orange light of the sunset. I look back at Mr. Layan with a clear, unspoken question. *Why are we here?*

"I know what the twelfth mark is," he says as he walks over, and I take a step back when I see the threatening look in his eyes. His words almost shock me in silence.

"What is it?" I ask hesitantly, and he laughs as he reaches into his cloak, pulling out a long, silver dagger. The memory of the vision comes flooding back to me, reminding me of Enzo's words.

"I'm going to kill that teacher for this."

"You don't want to do this, not really," I plead, putting my hands up, and he only laughs, dropping the dagger and using his air power to hold it in the air. I look at the dagger as he twirls it in circles, like it's a game and not that he is going to try to kill me. I can't die like this. I think back to what happened in my vision and know there's a chance Enzo will come for me. The future is never certain and changes all the time, but I have to believe he's coming.

"It's nothing personal, Miss Crowe. But, you're too powerful, and I won't let you destroy the world. The council and everyone who knows the truth of your power has gone mad keeping you alive," he says, and I instinctively put my hands up to stop the dagger as it flies through the air towards me. I call my protection mark, imagining the shield like I saw Locke do, but it's no use. The dagger goes straight through the ward and into my stomach, making me scream out in pain. Everything slows as I look down, watching as the dagger slides out of my stomach and flies away again.

"I am sorry for this, Miss Crowe, but there is a reason there is no one alive with twelve powers," I hear Mr. Layan say, and I force myself to look up as he raises his hand, shooting streams of fire around the room. I don't need to look around to see he is setting the whole hall on fire.

"You won't get away with this, they will know it's you," I gasp out, placing my hand on my stomach and pressing down as I struggle to keep standing from the pain.

"I don't plan to stay around and see, Miss Crowe. It doesn't matter in the end, as they will only think the rebels or someone else did this to you, not me," he says, his voice confident and cocky once more. The flames around the room grow fiercer. I watch in horror as he walks out of the room, pulling the door shut behind him, trapping me in with the fire and slowly building smoke. I slowly walk towards the door, feeling the heat from the flames, every movement sending pain through my stomach.

"Enzo," I breathe out when I see him open the door, his dark eyes meeting mine, and the fire in the room seems to reflect in his eyes. Black eyes and flame filled with anger. It's the last thought I have before everything goes black.

Chapter 26
KENZIE

urning, my marks are all burning. Vaguely aware of the sounds of screaming, I finally realise the tortured sounds are coming from my own throat. Twitching where I lie on the ground, I look up at the bright, shining plane of light above me. There are people gathered around in a circle, all dressed in marked, ceremonial robes. Their hoods are up and covering their faces. The pain radiating from my marks is unbearable . . . .

"Kenzie?" a voice says softly, but it's not coming from here.

A person steps forward towards the plane of light, and everyone standing around seems to lean forward in anticipation.

"Kenz, wake up," the voice speaks again, but it sounds closer this time.

My body thrashes around on the cold, hard ground. I need to stop them.

"Kenzie!" a different voice shouts, shaking me. My eyes flare open, and I look up at the people standing around me. I'm lying on my bed in Mr. Daniels' cabin. *How did I get here?*

The person with their hands on me is Logan. His forehead is creased in worry, and there is blood on his shirt. I look up and notice a few of them have blood on them. Enzo is the worst; his shirt looks soaked in it.

"Are you guys okay?" I croak. I try to sit up, but a pain slams through my stomach. I cry out from the pain and retreat down, my hand clutching at my middle.

"Shit, don't move, Kenz!" East says, resting a hand on my shoulder, as if to enforce my lack of moving. *No worries there, buddy. I am not going anywhere.*

"What happened?" I ask, my head feeling confusing. *There were people in a circle, or was that a dream?*

"You were stabbed, Mr. Layan is the main suspect. Enzo saw him fleeing the scene, and he hasn't been found anywhere since," Mr. Daniels explains. I try to get my head around that, a few images flicker through my head, but it's all still too distorted.

"Any reason nobody has healed me?" I ask, gesturing down at my stomach wrapped in bandages. I look across at the medical equipment. *Someone gave me stitches?*

"We tried," Enzo answers through gritted teeth.

"We think the dagger used to stab you was laced with marked powers," Locke says, sitting at the foot of the bed.

"How?" I ask, having not heard of that being possible before.

"We believe the dagger is one of the original artifacts we have from Ariziadia," Mr. Daniels answers. "We healed you the best we can, and we used human medicine combined with it where our powers wouldn't do the job. You will heal, but it will take a few days," he adds.

"Fuck it hurts," I mumble, resting my head back against the pillow.

The door crashes open, and all the guys move as one turning to face the entrant. They all visibly relax upon seeing who has entered.

"Why the hell did nobody tell me you brought her here?" Kelly screeches.

Silence from all the guys.

"I've been looking everywhere for where you could have taken her, since Enzo ran off to get Kenzie after my vision," she explains, moving across the room to me.

"Hey, Kells," I greet her, trying to manage a smile through the pain.

"You look awful," she says, reaching down to give me a hug. I wrap one arm around her back, returning the embrace.

"Thanks, just what I wanted to hear," I reply sarcastically, as she pulls away. She gives me a rueful smile and steps back, glaring at the men standing around me.

"Not one of you thought to call me?" she questions.

"We were busy," East says, gesturing to me.

"I could have helped," she replies, narrowing her eyes on him.

"We already had a few healers here, what more could you have done?" he asks.

"Guys, can you cut it out? You're here now, Kells. Thank you. I'm guessing your vision was of me being stabbed? You sent Enzo?" I ask. I look up for him, but notice Enzo must have crept out of the room at some point since Kelly walked in. Because he's sure as hell not here now, unless he's gained powers of invisibility. *The asshole just left?*

"He was there when I had my vision, I told him you were in trouble, and he was gone off to find you. I've never seen anyone run so fast," Kelly answers.

"He didn't run fast enough," East mutters, glaring at the open door. A hand rubs up and down my leg comfortingly. I look down and smile at Locke, who continues to rub his hand across my leg.

"He ran straight to her, he couldn't have gotten there quicker if he tried," Logan says, resting a hand on East's shoulder, but he shrugs it off.

"Fuck off. He should have called us. I was closer, I could have gotten there in time if he had called," he replies.

"She wouldn't have been alone in the first place had you not been kicked out from class for stripping," Locke snaps, standing up.

"You helped come up with that plan!" East shouts back at him. Locke opens his mouth to reply when a loud bang hits against the wall, grabbing all our attention.

"Enough! All of you, fucking get out and don't come back until you start acting like adults," Mr. Daniels snaps. His fist has dented the wall. *That must have hurt.* "Kelly, you may stay," he adds more softly. She nods and sits down on a chair next to the bed.

"Hey! I didn't do anything," Logan complains.

"Blame your brother for your removal," Mr. Daniels says dryly.

"Fuck's sake," he mutters, moving to leave the room after East and Locke.

"Would you mind leaving, too? I just want to be with my bestie," I say softly to Mr. Daniels. He frowns, but nods and leaves at my request, closing the door softly behind him.

"Why did you want to be alone?" Kelly asks, after a tense moment of silence.

"I had a dream while I was unconscious, but it was confused. I think it may have been a vision," I admit.

"And?" she asks, knowing there is more.

"I want you to try and see if there is more," I ask.

"I can't right this second, I'm wiped out from the vision of you being stabbed earlier. That really hurt," she mutters.

"You felt it?" I ask.

"Yeah. It was weird, in the vision it was as if I was you. I felt everything, and I mean everything. Gods, Kenzie that really fucking hurt, and the smoke was horrible. I could feel you choking on it as Enzo came in," she explains.

"That is weird. I'm sorry you had to feel that, Kells," I say, grabbing her hand.

"It's okay. I'm glad I did, Enzo got to you in time. You're gonna be okay," she says, a tear rolling down her face.

"Don't cry," I say, hearing the thickness in my own voice.

"My best friend almost died, and I felt it. I think I'm entitled to a few tears," she replies, more tears chasing the others.

"But, I'm fine, honestly. I'll be okay, you said so yourself," I reply, squeezing her hand.

"I know," she says softly. "But, I'll feel better once you are back on your feet. I'll try and look for your future later, but you know how unpredictable visions are," she says.

"I know, but it's worth a shot, right?" I ask.

"Worth a shot," she affirms, sitting back in her seat and stealing a blanket off the bottom of the bed.

"Getting comfy?" I question.

"Might as well, I'm not going anywhere," she answers, smiling at me. Her phone starts ringing, and she hands it over to me, as I give her a questioning look.

"I told Ryan," she says, and I groan, glaring at her as I answer the call.

"Hey, bro," I say, and I hear a big sigh of relief on the other end.

"Kennie, shit I was so worried. Are you okay?" he asks me, sounding stressed.

"Yeah, well kind of," I reply, trying not to move too much on the bed as my stomach is killing me.

"Has no one healed you yet?" he asks, picking up on something in my voice, I guess.

"The blade was laced with marked powers. They can't heal me completely, but I will get better soon," I tell him, and I hear him hit something.

"Shit. I should have been there or something. I have to go, Kennie, and I'm going to sort this all out," he tells me, and I frown, knowing there isn't much he can do.

"Is the council going to send your team out after Mr. Layan?" I ask, my voice comes out funny, and I grit my teeth from the pain in my stomach as I shift position.

"Not exactly, but don't worry about it," he says, making me want to worry about him even more. I rest my head back as everything starts to get a bit blurry. A roaring sound fills my ears.

"Here, let me," Kelly says, her voice sounding faded as she takes the phone from me. I can faintly hear her whispering to Ryan just as I fall asleep, but I'm already too far gone to catch the words.

Chapter 27

KENZIE

"*T*here's still been no signs of Mr. Layan," Mr. Daniels says, his voice void of emotion as he slips his phone back into his pocket. *Two weeks. It's been two fucking weeks since I was stabbed, and they haven't found him.* I had started my classes again after only a week. Thankfully, even without healing powers working fully, I had healed much faster than a human ever would.

Not so thankfully, Mr. Daniels had been making me take extra classes with him every single day since. I eye up his muscular frame leaning against his kitchen counter. The man is terrifyingly impressive. If I could even soak up a little of his abilities in fighting and defence, I would be happy. But, he wanted perfect. So, for three hours every day we have been sparring, using our magical abilities and a mixture of physical fighting. The amount I was getting my ass kicked was embarrassing. Especially since he'd said he was even going a little easier on me. When I told him to stop doing that yesterday . . . . *Damn I wish I'd kept my mouth shut.* The ache in my muscles is unreal.

"Are they even looking," I mutter.

"Yes, of course, they are looking; they have practically the entire council out looking. He seems to have planned his getaway meticulously, Miss Crowe," he answers.

I shove my cornflakes away, my appetite gone.

"I have protection class, and it's my first one as I couldn't get to the others with training and everything, so I should go," I say, and he looks over at me, a worried frown appearing on his handsome face.

"You're not going to be late for class?" he jokes, making me smile slightly as he tries to cheer me up, but when I place my hand on my stomach, feeling the slightly raised scar, that I will always have, through my thin t-shirt, my smile disappears. I grab my phone and walk out, waving goodbye to Mr. Daniels. I walk towards the school and use the academy app to find my way to the right classroom. The corridors are surprisingly quiet. When I find the classroom on the second floor, I knock before opening the door and walking in. The room is empty, and I check my phone once more, seeing that I'm in the right place and sit down on one of the chairs that are placed in rows in the middle of the room. I hear the bell ring a few seconds later and look up as the twins walk into the room, smiling when they see me. Locke sits on my left, sliding his arm around my chair, and Logan sits on my other side, his hand brushing mine.

"Early to class, I'm shocked," Locke whispers as five more students walk into the room.

"It is shocking," Logan agrees.

"I'm not late to everything," I say, and they both laugh. I go to ask Logan what he's doing here, when a teacher walks into the room and slams the door shut, making herself jump. The teacher looks in her mid-thirties with long, blonde hair, a sweet face that makes her look young, and she is wearing a long jumper and jeggings. She looks beautiful, but normal, it's shocking compared to the teachers in this place.

"Silly door," she mumbles, walking into the classroom and dropping her bag on the floor. She spots both twins sitting in the room and frowns. "Which one of you isn't meant to be in here?" she asks. They both shrug and keep their mouths shut. She sighs and looks around the rest of the room.

"Fine, both of you stay. So, hi everyone, except you. You're new?" she asks me, smiling as she walks over and offers me her hand to shake. I shake her hand as I speak.

"I'm Mackenzie, and I haven't been able to come to class before this." She nods as understanding washes over face.

"Miss Perfect with twelve marks can't even defend herself against an old teacher," I hear whispered from behind me. The comment is met with laughter as my cheeks go red. It wasn't like that, but this is all I've been hearing all week in my classes. Luckily, the guys are always with me and defend me, even Enzo did despite the fact he isn't talking to me since he saved my life. I remember in the vision how he kissed my forehead, how close we got on that sofa and now nothing. It was beyond frustrating and confusing.

"Dickhead," Locke mutters angrily and stands up, lifting his hand and sending the two students flying into the air and landing on their asses across the room.

"Nice one, twin," Logan laughs, sliding his hand into mine.

"What the hell?" one of the guys says as he stands up, offering a hand to his friend. Locke goes to step forward when the teacher puts her hand in front of him, and a large ward appears, spreading around Locke and keeping him trapped in place. I don't think Locke is really trapped as he doesn't fight it, but looks down at me.

"Locke, or Logan—whichever one you are—that was not nice," she says to him, before turning toward the student who was whispering. "But, neither were your comments to Mackenzie. I want everyone to sit down, and if I hear any more comments or use of the air mark, then I will kick you all out," she says firmly, smoothing down her dress and sighing.

"Now, I'm Miss Ash, but you can call me Tia," she says to me gently, as she lowers the ward around Locke, and he grumpily returns to his seat. I hear the other guys sit down behind me as Tia carries on talking.

"So, in previous classes we have been testing our protection ward and going over the various uses we have for it," she tells us.

"I want you to pair up and carry on the testing we have been doing in the last few lessons. Mackenzie, I will pair up with you, and we shall start at the beginning," she tells me, and I nod, standing up, as everyone else does, and letting go of Logan's hand. I walk over to Tia, and she gestures for me to stand in front of her.

"So, have you used your protection ward before?" she asks me.

"Yes, I used it to block a pain mark being used on me. And then, I used it again when Mr. Layan . . .," I let my words drift off, and she nods, a sympathetic look crossing over her face.

"I heard what weapon he used, wards cannot protect against mark-laced weapons,"

"I figured that one out," I whisper.

"Also, Mr. Layan is very well-trained with his ten marks, and you still survived. If anything, you should be proud of yourself. I don't believe I would survive a fight against him," she tells me gently, and I can't do anything but nod at her.

"Well, why don't you show me how you used the ward before?" she asks, and I close my eyes, imagining the protection ward and holding my hand up. The moment I start feeling my hand going warm, I imagine the look on Mr. Layan's face as my ward failed and that dagger went through my stomach. I remember the pain, the fire, and the smoke. The feeling of helplessness as I choked.

"I can't," I stumble out, dropping my hand and turning around. I'm gone, running out the door and down the corridor as I hear Locke and Logan shouting my name behind me. I used protection fine with Mr. Daniels, so why can't I do it on my own? *Why do I keep remembering that night?*

"Kenz," Logan says as he catches up with me, grabbing onto my arm to stop me running anymore. When I look up at him, he pulls me into his arms and hugs me. Seconds later, I feel Locke rubbing a hand down my back as I try to get my breathing under control.

"What happened?" Logan asks me gently, and I shake my head, not wanting to talk about it at all.

"I have an idea. You need to relax a little, all work and no play can't be good for you."

"Where should we go?" Logan asks Locke.

"The restricted place? It could be fun?" Locke replies, and I let Logan take my hand, walking me down the corridor. Locke takes my other hand, entwining our fingers.

"Where are we going?" I ask, feeling stressed and tired. Locke is right, it's been too much training with Mr. Daniels, all my lessons, and then getting only five minutes a day to see anyone else before collapsing in bed.

"Well, I may have a key to the entrance pool of the academy," Locke says, pulling out his set of keys and flashing me an old-looking one. I laugh despite my mood, and he nods his head towards the big doors that lead to the pool.

"What on earth are we going to do down there?" I ask, and it's Logan that answers in a whisper as Locke opens the door.

"Skinny dipping, what else?"

"You, me, and Locke naked," I blurt out as he moves closer and shocks me by pressing his lips gently against mine before pulling away before it can be classed as a real kiss.

"That's the plan," he says, chuckling at my red cheeks and little smile.

"Quick," Locke says and opens the door slightly, so we can slide in and stops my imagination from going into overdrive about the thought of seeing them both naked. Locke turns on the flashlight on his phone as we walk down the steep steps and I look down, seeing a lump of fabric at the bottom of the steps.

"What's that?" I ask, but the twins don't answer me as they both tense up. Logan quickly pushes me gently behind him as Locke steps closer. *What don't they want me to see?* I look around Logan's shoulder, and my eyes focus and take in the body at the bottom of the steps. I take an instant step back when I see the familiar white, long hair and black cloak, but then I notice the blood around his neck and all over his hair.

Mr. Layan is dead.

I spot a piece of paper in his hand. As much as I hate the man for what he did, I don't want to see him dead like this. He deserved to die, but not having his throat slit and used to carry a message.

"What does the note say?" I ask as Locke steps closer and looks around before kneeling next to Mr. Layan, pulling the note from his hand. Locke comes over giving me a worried look as he shows me the note. My heart almost stops as I read the name at the top.

"It's addressed to me," I whisper, flipping the note over and reading the message on the other side.

Miss Crowe,
A present for you.
We shall meet soon,
—A Friend.

"What kind of friend leaves you a dead body?" Logan asks, having read the note over my shoulder.

"Not the kind of friend I'd like to keep," I reply, feeling sick to my stomach.

"I'll call Mr Daniels, you get Kenzie back to the cabin," Locke says to his brother.

"Why are we leaving?" I ask as Logan already starts to tug me back up the stairs.

"A man who attempted to kill you shows up dead, and you're the one to find the body—in a place you shouldn't even be able to get into. Who do you think they'll consider as a suspect?"

"Shit," I mutter, seeing his point.

"Come on, Locke and Mr. Daniels will take care of it. But as far as anyone else is concerned, you never saw that body. Okay, Kenzie?" he says, hurrying me out the door. I stare back at the door as we walk away from it. "Are we clear?" he asks, sliding a hand into mine.

"Crystal," I answer. I screw up the note in my other hand and shove it into my pocket, wishing I really hadn't seen the body.

Chapter 28

KENZIE

I instantly regret the decision to have breakfast with my friends in the dining hall as soon as I walk in. Eyes follow me everywhere I walk, and silence or whispers are all I am greeted with. *Great. News travels fast in the academy.* I grab my food, then spot East, Kelly, and Enzo at our usual table and make my way over.

Taking the seat between Easton and Kelly, I silently push my food around my plate. Other than a few hushed hellos as I sit down, our table keeps to the quiet that encompasses the rest of the room. I shovel some food in my mouth, not really tasting it.

The silence is broken by the sound of laughter and chatting as the twins walk in, acting completely oblivious to the tension in the room. It has the effect of a popped balloon, suddenly everyone is talking again. They chat loudly as they grab their food and make their way across to us. They take their seats at the table, across from me and either side of Enzo.

"You all look cheerful today," Locke says, tucking into his food like he doesn't have a care in the world.

"Yeah, because dead bodies just fill us with cheer," I mutter.

"He tried to kill you, Kenzie. I can't say I'm filled with sadness," he replies, taking a big bite of toast.

"Still, I don't think that after we found—"

"So, Kenzie, what classes do you have today?" Kelly quickly asks, changing the subject. I'm about to ask her what her deal is, when I realise what I'd almost said. *Shit. I almost blew the 'who really found the body secret' the very next day.* The only people who know are Mr. Daniels, and the people sitting around this table with me right now. *I need to keep it that way.*

"Err . . . I only have earth class today, as air is cancelled . . . the normal teacher is still sick. Apparently, they're one of those people who reject marked healing," I answer.

"Who would reject healing?" Kelly asks, a frown crossing her face.

"I'm not sure, but after having healing not work properly on my stomach wound, I will never take it for granted again," I reply.

"You up for cutting class today, Kenz?" Logan asks.

"Yes, because that went so well last time," I whisper.

"You need a break, you're exhausted," he says softly, reaching for my hand across the table.

"Yeah, maybe I do need a break, but it can wait till this afternoon. If any of you have a free period, do you wanna come over to the cabin and hang out? I know Mr. Daniels is elsewhere today," I ask everyone.

"I have a class, but I'm more than happy to skip it," Locke says.

"Count me in," Logan adds.

"I was meant to be in air with you, so you know I'm free," East says, giving me a small smile.

"I'll be there, Crowe," Enzo answers, standing. "But, I've got something to do right now, I'll see you all later," he adds, and then turns and leaves, walking quickly and with purpose. He's gone before we can ask him where he's off to. I turn to Kelly for her answer.

"Well?" I ask, smiling.

"I'm free lesson-wise, I have plans, but can come later," Kelly says softly.

"Plans?" I question.

"Don't sound so surprised," she says quickly.

"What are you doing?" I ask her, the look on her face making me concerned.

"Who are you, my keeper?" she snaps, standing up.

"Don't snap at Kenzie like that," Locke says to Kelly. *Crap, what is even happening here?*

"Kelly, what's up with you?" I ask her, not really understanding the abrupt change in her behaviour.

"Nothing, I just have plans. I'm sorry for snapping. I'll see you later," she stumbles out as she turns to leave.

"Kelly, wait up!" I say standing.

"Just leave me alone, Kenz. I have something to sort out," she replies. She quickly makes her way out of the dining hall as I take my seat again.

"That was weird," East comments.

"No fucking kidding," I mumble, staring at the door. *What is up with her recently?* I feel East nudge me gently in the side.

"Finish your breakfast, Kenz," he says gently.

I push the food around my plate, making a show of taking a few bites so as not to concern the guys, but the food is tasteless. I look up at the door again. *I will find out what's going on with you, Kelly. Even if I have to follow you to do it.*

Chapter 29
KENZIE

*a*fter making my excuses to the guys about why I'm going to be late, I sneak off in search of Kelly. Luckily, it isn't too hard to find her. I spot her making her way hurriedly across the courtyard by her dorm building. *Gotcha.*

I follow at a distance, trying to keep out of her sight. I feel a bit like a creeper following my best friend around, but I know when something is up. There is most definitely something going on with my best friend right now, and I intend to find out what. I follow her quietly, trying to figure out where the hell she is going. It only becomes clear when I spot the building up ahead, the abandoned dorm building.

Who is she meeting here?

She slinks around the back of the building, and in through the back door that has again been left ajar. I wait a few minutes, hoping she's moved within the building enough to not hear me follow her inside. Creeping as quietly as possible to the door, and slipping into the building. I try to focus on what's around me, but it's so dark in here. *Damn it, why didn't I bring my phone to use as a light*? I wait for a minute, allowing my eyes to adjust to the darkness. I slowly step further into the building, doing a quiet search of the lower floor, before determining that Kelly must have gone upstairs. *Fuck, I hope they don't creak.*

Moving quietly up the stairs, I tentatively place my foot on each next step, only slowly adding my weight. Eventually, I make it to the top of the stairs. Only having taken three steps away from the stairs, I freeze when I hear a voice. Kelly's voice.

"I cannot believe what you're doing," Kelly's voice says.

"It's for the greater good, you should understand," a man's voice replies. A familiar voice. I move toward the voices.

"The greater good? They killed a man!" Kelly snaps.

"A man that tried to kill your best friend," he replies.

"Murder is wrong, no matter who it is you're killing. They could have handed him over to the council and had him tried legally," Kelly argues. My heart is thudding in my chest as I reach the door at the end of the corridor, where the voices appear to be coming from.

"I didn't kill him," he replies.

"You may as well have. You helped dump the body

here, I saw it!" she snaps. *Wait, what? Kelly saw the people leave the body?*

"Nobody saw us," he grunts.

"I saw it in a vision. I saw you put the note into his hand for Kenzie, how could you do that to her!" she asks.

"He tried to kill her. He deserved it," he replies. *His voice—It can't be.*

"You can't be serious. You know I love you, but how am I meant to keep this to myself?" Kelly whispers. *Kelly loves him? There has to be a mistake here, surely.* I move to try and sneak a peek through the crack in the door.

"I want us to be together, Kelly, but it's too dangerous right now. We will be together soon, and none of this will matter. Once his plan is in motion, we won't have to hide anymore," he says softly, an almost promising tone to his voice. I catch a glimpse of the man with his hood up standing next to Kelly, he's placed a hand on her cheek. I feel sick to my stomach, I can't watch this.

"I can't . . . you can't trust them. What if they are going to hurt her? I heard the rumours, that they were here for her the day they attacked," Kelly says.

"They're not going to hurt Kennie, they need her. You should know I wouldn't let them hurt her," he says, sounding a little offended by the idea.

"Why do they need her?" Kelly asks.

"I can't tell you that right now, Kelly, but it'll all be clear soon. Just trust me," he pleads.

"I-I don't know if I can," she replies so quietly I

barely catch it. I watch through the crack in the door as he pulls down his hood, his back to me. He leans down, and they kiss. *How did I not see this coming?*

"Trust me," he says again. He turns slightly, and I dart back, afraid he'll spot me. I back away, not able to listen to this conversation anymore.

My brother. My best friend is in love with my brother.

And even better, he's involved with Mr. Layan's murder.

This cannot be happening.

I make my way back out of the old dorm building as quietly, but quickly, as possible. Once I'm outside, I run. I run straight through the woods and toward the cabin, needing to get far away from there. A body crashes into mine, knocking, and then pinning, me to the ground. *Fuck.* I look up at Enzo's face staring down at mine.

"Why the fuck are you running through the woods? I shouted for you six times, and you just kept running!" he snaps.

"You shouted?" I whisper.

"Well, duh," he replies sarcastically, his face painted with annoyance.

"I'm sorry," I mumble, trying to wriggle out of his hold.

"Hey, don't go timid on me, Crowe. I was just messing around. Are you okay?" he asks, brushing my hair out of my face.

I look up into his dark eyes and shake my head.

"What's wrong?" he questions softly.

"I don't know who to trust," I reply quietly, letting out a sigh.

"You know you can trust me, right?" he says.

"Trust you?" I ask, a small smile crossing my lips.

"Always," he replies, and then he closes the distance between us, pressing his lips to mine. I gasp from shock, not expecting the kiss. He goes to pull away, and I slide a hand around his neck and pull him back, returning the kiss.

He tangles his hand in my hair, deepening the kiss between us, before pulling away and quickly standing back up. I can't help but feel like the kiss was over way too quickly.

"Come on then, the others will wonder where you've gotten to if we're late," he says, no sign in his voice that what had just happened, had happened.

"Um, okay?" I reply, slowly getting to my feet. He leads the way back to the cabin, and as I follow him, I can't help but wonder what has him so hot and cold. One minute he's talking to me, flirting with me, and now, kissing me. And then another, he's ignoring me and acting as if there is nothing at all between us. Shaking my head to myself, I resign myself to the fact that Enzo is confusing, but that I have bigger fish to worry about.

Enzo may be hot and cold, but Kelly loves Ryan.

Ryan is an accomplice in a murder.

And, the rebels need me for something.

When did life get this messed up?

Chapter 30

KENZIE

"*O*kay that's it. What is wrong, Kenz? You've been ignoring us all and staring at the window for the last hour," Locke asks me as I stand up and walk over to the window, looking out at the dark forest. *How long is Kelly going to be?* I can't focus on the movie the guys chose or the food that East brought. All I can think about is how my brother and Kelly are together. I think back to all the times he texted me about Kelly. The way she blushed when I guessed she was with someone, but didn't tell me anything. It was right there all along, and I never guessed. *I'm such an idiot for not realising.*

"Kenzie," Enzo says firmly, and I turn to look at him and all the guys who are staring at me. East turns off the movie as Enzo gets up and walks over to me. The twins give me worried glances, and I know I'm going to have to make something up or tell them the

CECE ROSE AND G. BAILEY

truth. I glance at East, wondering if he knew, considering he is Ryan's best friend. Surely, he must have known something about them.

"What's going on?" he asks, rubbing a hand down my arm, but I don't get a chance to reply as the cabin door is knocked on once before the door is opened, and Kelly walks in. The moment I see her all I can think of is how she kissed Ryan, how she said she loved him. She's been there with him all this time, and it's been ages. The flushed cheeks, and messed up buttons on her coat suggest she is sleeping with him, too. She knows my brother is working with the rebels and knows my brother helped kill Mr. Layan. *What else has she been hiding from me?*

"Hey, I'm sorry about earlier, I was just stressed," she says as she starts to take her coat off.

"Are you feeling better now?" I snap, knowing my brother has made her feel better. She stops undoing her coat to stare at me.

"What's your problem?" she asks me, her eyes widening as she takes in how angry I am. If looks could kill, I doubt she'd be standing.

"Oh, I don't know, Kelly. Perhaps it's the fact my best friend is fucking my brother," I say, and there's silence in the room as I stare at her. She nods at me, her shoulders dropping.

"How long have you known? How did you find out?" she asks.

"Since I followed you and saw you kissing him through a window earlier tonight," I tell her.

"Did you hear anything we said?" she asks, and I

212

glance around the room, seeing all the guys watching us with worried glances, but they are smart enough not to say anything. I can't say anything about the rebels and my brother in front of them all, it's just not smart. They wouldn't trust her around me ever again, and I need to find a way to get my brother and Kelly out of this mess. I'm mad, but they're still two of the people I care about the most.

"Nothing. Once I saw you, I didn't want to stay for the show," I answer.

"Look, I'm sorry, but I love him. I've always liked him, growing up, but last Christmas, it became something more. Then we started texting and meeting up," she says, her voice drifting off as I walk around her towards the door and hold it open.

"How can I ever trust you again? You're meant to be my friend, and you've been lying to me for months. I just can't deal with you, with this, right now. Can you leave?" I ask her, watching as she wipes a few tears away and walks away from me. She stops in the doorway and looks back at me.

"You can't help who you fall in love with, you should know that, Kenz. Don't hate me for loving your brother, I couldn't help it. I am sorry I lied to you," she tells me and then leaves. I watch her walk away and wrap my arms around myself. I don't trust her because she still didn't tell me about the rebels and everything that happened. I can't help but hope she comes to me later and says something. *Maybe she just didn't want the guys to hear?*

"Kenz?" East says coming over to me, shutting the

door and pulling me into his arms. I rest my head on his chest and hug him back.

"Did you know?" I ask East, and he rubs his hands down my back.

"No idea. Ryan said he was dating someone he met at Christmas, but he never said who. I guessed it was someone he works with."

"I just don't get why she didn't tell me. I mean, I wouldn't have been against them being together, but to lie to me all this time?" I ask, but don't want an answer, and East seems to realise it.

"Maybe she was scared she would lose your friendship?" I hear Locke say, and I pull away from East to walk over to the sofa and sit next to him. I look over at Enzo, who is leaning against the window.

"I want to get drunk again, can we find wherever Mr. Daniels hid the vodka?" I ask him. He smirks at me.

"Under the kitchen sink, behind the cleaning stuff. There should be Vodka, whiskey, and possibly some rum," he answers.

"How do you know that?" Locke questions as he and Logan wander into the kitchen to check. Sure enough, they walk back in with vodka, whiskey, and half a bottle of rum.

"I've been down here a few times before Kenzie moved in, he always has some extra down there," he answers.

"Are you sure we should be drinking this? You're not eighteen yet, Miss Crowe," East says mockingly, his impression of Mr. Daniel's voice is eerie. I shrug.

"A week isn't going to make much of a difference," I reply, snagging the bottle of rum from Logan.

"It's your birthday next week?" Locke asks, his eyebrows raised.

"Shit, it is next Wednesday, isn't it?" East mutters, before taking a swig from one of the bottles.

"Why didn't you say anything?" Logan asks, snagging the bottle back from East.

"I guess between being stabbed, all the training, and Mr. Layan turning up dead, a birthday party didn't seem appropriate," I answer with a small smile.

"Screw that," Locke says.

"Definitely screw that," Logan reiterates.

"I hereby call this an early celebration of Kenzie's birthday," East says, snatching the bottle back again and raising it as if in toast. "Happy early birthday, Kenz," he adds and then takes a swig. I follow suit, and so does Locke, who's holding the other bottle. East and Locke pass their bottles to Logan and Enzo, who both take a drink, too.

"Let me grab some glasses," I say, standing up from the sofa. I make my way into the kitchen area and grab five glasses and attempt not to drop them as I wander back to the sofa. I place the glasses onto the coffee table and slide back onto my seat.

"You made that look so difficult, Kenzie," Logan says teasingly.

"I didn't want to drop them, okay?" I reply.

"You weren't walking on a tightrope," he replies.

"Not everyone was blessed with coordination. I sucked at sports in the human school I went to," I say.

"You went to a human school?" Enzo asks curiously.

"Yeah I went to the local comprehensive school. My mum thought it would be good for me to mix with human kids as well as Marked, I guess. I ended up loving a few of the human subjects, though. I wanted to go to University next year, but I had to let go of that dream because of well, marked powers and all," I say, sighing.

"What did you want to do?" East asks, sliding down onto the sofa next to me.

"I'm not completely sure to be honest. There were a few things I enjoyed. I had to leave my A levels half way through, though, so not much chance now," I say bitterly. Even I'm shocked at how bitter my voice sounds.

"That sucks," Locke says.

"Can't you go back and do it later?" Logan asks.

"I could, but I guess I'll just get a normal marked job. Maybe I'll teach or be a healer? Hell, they'll probably offer me a job at the council just because of my stupid marks," I answer.

"There are some marked who take jobs in human society," East says gently. I shake my head, pushing the foolish ideas away. I wasn't going to be a normal human, I wasn't born to be that.

"It's okay, I think since being marked with all twelve I've accepted the fact my life is going to be different to what I thought it would be before," I reply. I catch the concerned looks on the guys faces and decide that's enough moping for now. "Ugh, sorry guys. Total downer on my own early birthday party. Let's play a drinking game, shall we?" I ask, leaning forward and pouring drinks into all the glasses.

"What are we gonna play?" Locke asks, a roguish smile on his face. I think for a moment.

"Well, there's the card game ones, but I'm not sure we have a deck here . . .," I trail off, trying to figure out where, if at all, Mr. Daniels would leave a deck of cards.

"We could always play a game that doesn't require cards," Logan suggests.

"Like what?" I ask.

"Never have I ever?" he answers, a matching roguish smile taking over his face as is on his twin's. East and Enzo groan.

"What?" I ask, looking at them.

"Logan or Locke always suggest it, they're terrible," East answers.

"You're only saying that because you're a man-whore that clearly gets drunk too easily," Locke says, downing half of his drink. *Man-whore?* I look across at the four guys sitting with me. I really don't want to know all the things they've done, knowing the kind of statements that are normally made in this game.

"Maybe this isn't such a clever idea?" I suggest.

"Kenzie, what dirty secrets are you trying to hide from us?" Logan teases. I laugh so hard and suddenly, a snort escapes. I pull a mortified face as my eyes meet East's who laughs at me.

"Yeah, not so many dirty secrets here," I reply, trying to swiftly move on from the snort laughter.

"Did you just snort?" Locke asks. *Or not.*

"Just a little," I reply, trying to laugh it off. I take a big drink from my glass of rum.

"Well, wasn't that adorable?" Enzo says.

"Please shut up now," I plead, looking between them all.

"Fine, we'll shut up, but we're playing a drinking game," Logan replies.

"I know where the cards are," Enzo adds, moving away from the window and heading for Mr. Daniels' room. I watch the bedroom door, waiting for Enzo to return.

"The fact you know where stuff is in Mr. Daniels' bedroom is beyond creepy," I mutter, as Enzo walks back in with the deck of cards.

"Hey now, don't try and draw attention away from the fact you are well and truly about to get smashed losing this game, Mackenzie," he says, laying the cards out across the coffee table.

"What are we playing?" I ask.

"You're going to ride the bus," he answers.

"Ride the bus?" I ask quizzically, looking at the cards faced down across the table. He flips the first card over, a seven.

"Which card on the next row and will it be higher or lower, Mackenzie?" he questions.

"The one closer to me, and Higher?" I guess. He flips over the card. A six.

"Drink up, Kenz," Logan says, nudging my drink towards me. I look at the seven rows of cards that I'm guessing I have to make it through.

"I have to get them all right to finish, right?" I ask, the dread already pooling in my stomach. Enzo nods.

"Let's hope you can hold your booze better than the twins can," East says, throwing an arm over my shoulders. I sink into him and take a sip of my drink, feeling the warmth of his body against mine warm me outside, as the drink warms me from inside.

Enzo replaces the first two cards that were flipped for me to start again.

"Ready?"

Ready to guess them all wrong and get blindly drunk? Yeah sure, why not.

"Bring it," I mutter. He flips the new first card over.

Chapter 31

KENZIE

*W*aking up sandwiched between the twins probably would have been nice if it wasn't for Logan's snores in my ear. I force open my eyes, despite the banging already settling into my head and look down. *At least, I'm still dressed. I've had enough awkward nudity recently to last a lifetime.*

I roll over closer to Locke to escape Logan's soft snoring, only to find his gentle snores match his twin's. *Great.* I slide down to the bottom of the bed and climb off, coming to a halt when I realise where I am. *Shit, why are we sleeping in Mr. Daniels' room?* I look around at the practically bare room. *No wonder Enzo found the cards so easily, there's barely anything in here.*

Slinking quietly out the door, I creep through the cabin, noting a sleeping Enzo on the sofa as I pass him by. I reach my bedroom, and slip inside, closing the door softly behind me. I turn to face the room and let out a half-scream, smacking my hand over my mouth to cut it off before I wake anyone.

Holy shit.

Easton Black is lying naked in my bed.

Completely fucking naked.

I stand there gaping, my mouth opening and closing like a fish. After a few seconds, I realise he's asleep, the slight movement of his sculpted chest rising and falling. *At least, I didn't wake him.* I can't help but run my eyes across him one last time, and then turn to leave.

"Morning, Kenzie," East's voice rumbles from behind me as I reach for the door handle. *Shit.*

"Morning, East," I choke out.

"Enjoy the view?" he asks.

"View?"

"Don't play innocent now, Kenz. I know you looked," he teases.

"I didn't—"

"You're more than welcome to continue your perusal," he adds, cutting off my denial. I turn around, deliberately keeping my eyes on his face.

"I don't know what you mean, East, but I do need to grab some clothes. Maybe you could do the same?" I suggest, walking across to the chest of drawers. I rifle through them hastily grabbing underwear, jeans, and a black camisole top. I feel East before I hear him, his hot breath on my neck, as his hands slide around my waist.

"You could always take some clothes off instead?" he suggests, whispering into my ear. I shiver, feeling

221

the tremble run right through me. Dropping the clothes in my hands to the floor, I turn around to face him, caged between his body and the chest of drawers. He slides a hand behind my neck and pulls me toward him, stopping just before our lips can meet. I lean forward and close the gap between us, gently kissing him as I slide my own hands around his back, feeling his muscles tense under my touch. The kiss doesn't stay gentle for long. East deepens it as he moves his hands down my body and then slips them back around me, lifting me on top of the chest of drawers. I wrap my legs around him as he presses in close, feeling every inch of him pushed up against me. He moves his hands over my shirt, teasing as he runs his fingertips over the edges of my bra.

I reach up, running my fingers through his soft, light-brown hair. He pulls his lips away from mine, and kisses down my neck, and down to my chest. He tugs my shirt down, continuing to trail kisses and gentle bites across me. The sound of something being knocked over in the next room drags me to my senses.

"Shit, East. We've got to stop," I say, pulling his head back up to look at me.

"Why?" he asks confused. I turn my head to the closed door, knowing Enzo, Logan, and Locke are on the other side. *With the dynamic of whatever relationship there is between us not decided, it wouldn't be fair for me to just do this, would it? That's not even including my feelings for Mr. Daniels, which are utterly pointless anyway.* Sighing, I turn back to East.

"I just can't. The others . . .," I begin, but trail off.

Unable to complete the sentence. I chew on my lip nervously.

"It's okay, Kenz. The twins know how I feel, and I know how they feel," he says, running a soothing hand up and down my back. I stay silent, not able to form the words I want to say. "Enzo too, huh?" he adds gently. I nod mutely. *That's half of it anyway.* "We can sort that all out first, then. There's no rush," he says, dropping a gentle kiss onto my forehead before untangling our bodies and stepping away. He pulls on his boxers and jeans before stepping back to me and kissing me hard. He steps back again and looks at me expectantly, waiting for me to say something.

"I better get ready for class," I reply nervously, jumping down off the chest of drawers.

"Yeah, because you showing up late for a class is completely unheard of. Wouldn't want to ruin your stellar reputation as a star pupil now, would you?" he says teasingly. And just like that, the tension is broken. I laugh.

"Hey! I'm not late to all my classes," I grumble.

"Really?" he asks.

"Yeah, I show up to Mr. Daniel's classes on time. I can't really make up excuses for being late when I live in the cabin with him," I reply jokingly, grabbing the fresh set of clothes I'd dropped to change into. "What's the time, anyway?" I ask as I walk towards the door to head to the bathroom for a quick shower.

"Well, you're already thirty minutes late to fire class," he says.

"Wait, already thirty minutes late?" I ask, groaning. Just great.

"Luckily, it's your favourite teacher, Kenz," he replies sarcastically, as I exit the room.

Shit. Miss Tinder is going to kill me.

Chapter 32

KENZIE

"*M*r. Daniels, I'm sure Miss Crowe will be here any moment," I hear Miss Tinder say as I walk into fire class. The whole class is sitting, talking or playing on their phones, when I walk in. They all stop to look at me with surprise. *Hey, it's not like I don't turn up to my classes, I'm just usually late.* I glance at the clock on the wall. *Maybe not this late though.*

"Miss Crowe, this is completely unacceptable. You are forty-five minutes late, and I don't know why I'm not surprised when I should be. Honestly, it's like you believe your twelve marks make you impervious to the rules of this academy," she turns to me as she speaks, but my eyes are locked on Mr. Daniels who shakes his head as he looks me over. He looks stressed, today, with his brown hair messy and looks like he has run his fingers through it a few times and his clothes are wrinkled which is unlike him. He's also missing his glasses, which are normally only off during our training.

"Sorry I'm late," Enzo says walking into the room after me and not even looking at Mr. Daniels or Miss Tinder as he takes his seat. Miss Tinder doesn't even look his way, or care that he is late. Just me.

"Outside, now, Miss Crowe," Mr. Daniels says, just as I go to sit down.

I turn to see him walking out of the classroom and look over at Miss Tinder.

"Go, and don't be long," she tells me. I nod and walk out of the classroom, pulling the door closed behind me. I turn to see Mr. Daniels standing in the middle of the empty corridor with his arms crossed and an expression that makes me want to hide. *Shit.*

"So . . .," I ask, wondering why he dragged me out here and is giving me this look.

"Miss Crowe . . . I just don't even know where to start with you," he says and runs a hand through his hair as he watches me.

"Erm quietly? My head is banging," I sigh, placing my hand against my head and knowing I should have grabbed some food or something earlier. I didn't stop when I jumped into the shower and then ran to class. I haven't had time to even think about everything that happened with Kelly and Ryan. I try to nip that thought in the bud. I can't even think about it at the moment, as all I want to do is find Kelly and talk to her.

As I watch Mr. Daniels walking over to me, I get

what Kelly was talking about when she said you don't choose who you fall for. *You really don't.* Mr. Daniels stops in front of me, placing his hand on my head, and I feel him healing me before stepping away.

"Why did you heal me?" I ask him, relief spreading over me now that my head doesn't hurt anymore.

"So that I can shout at you for getting drunk with your friends last night in my house," he says, and I mentally cringe. *Shit, he must have come back at some point.* When I don't say anything, he continues. "I came back from the meeting I told you about, to find you dancing on the coffee table," he tells me. A flashback of last night runs through my mind.

"At least, I had my clothes on, or from what I can remember," I say, making him groan and look at me closely as I smile at him. We both start laughing after an awkward silence, and he shakes his head.

"What am I going to do with you, Miss Crowe?" he asks, stepping closer to me and placing his hand on my arm.

"What do you want to do, Mr. Daniels?" I ask, not able to stop the tempting words leaving my lips.

"You don't want to know," he whispers, his face inches away from mine. I can smell the body wash he uses, the same stuff I used quickly in the shower this morning.

"What's your first name?" I ask him, not moving as we stand close to each other, our lips inches apart, and my hand moves to rest on his chest without me thinking about it. It just feels natural.

227

"It's—" he starts to say, and then he suddenly jumps away when the door is opened behind me.

"I need to start my lesson, Mr. Daniels," Miss Tinder's voice says behind me, her voice chipped and annoyed as I turn to see her looking between us.

"We will finish speaking about this later, Miss Crowe," he says, his tone back to the cold and emotionless tone that I'm used to. I nod, walking back into the classroom and taking the empty seat next to Enzo as he smirks at me.

"What did Mr. Dead Serious want this morning?" Enzo asks me.

"He came back at some point last night and saw me dancing on the table," I tell him, and he laughs, making several people turn to look at us. Miss Tinder slams the door shut after she walks into the room, and everyone goes quiet. I glance behind me when I hear someone cough and see Stella sitting with her feet on the table at the back of class and glaring at me. *Just great, why is she here?*

"So, class, *now* that the disruptions are out of the way, we shall begin. We have been studying how to control your fire mark. It's very easy to make a large fire and much harder to make only a small amount, like lighting a candle without melting the entire thing," Miss Tinder says after clapping her hands. I look down at the three candles in holders on the table in front of me, and it makes sense what we are going to be doing now.

"Please spend the next hour lighting the candles. There are spares at the front if you melt yours. Once you are done, you may leave and have a study period," she tells the class. That's all the encouragement they need as some start trying to light the candles straight away, and I watch them melt them, the clumsy rush doing them no good. I look over as Enzo wipes a hand across the tips of the candles in front of him, lighting them all perfectly before leaning back in his seat and shrugging.

"Come on, you can do this. Then we can go and get food," he says, waiting for me, and it's kind of sweet from the bad boy who pretends to be asshole-like. I call my fire mark and concentrate on lighting just the candles. I open my eyes to see nothing has happened. *Maybe I was thinking too small?*

"Mackenzie, focus on the tips of the candles and just lighting those. The idea isn't to just think fire, it's to focus on what you want the fire to do. Fire can be controlled with your mind before you let it out with your mark," Enzo whispers gently, and I give him a thankful look. I hover my hand over the first candle and imagine the wick catching fire as I call my mark. When I open my eyes, the candle is lit, and I quickly do the others.

"Thank you," I say as Enzo stands up and smirks down at me.

"It was nothing, I just want food and not to be sitting here all day, or to have to stop you from setting the room on fire, again," he says and walks out. I laugh and follow him out, seeing Miss Tinder nod at me as she looks at my candles.

"Impressive, Miss Crowe," she comments and then

looks back at the paperwork in front of her. When I walk out of the classroom, I see Stella talking to Enzo. They are standing closely together, and I watch in disgust when she places both her perfectly manicured hands on his chest. I want to snap the purple-tipped nails straight off her. Enzo steps back, but unfortunately for him, there's a wall behind his back, and she boxes him in as she moves closer again. They are arguing, and I don't think as I walk over, stepping next to Enzo and reaching a hand to the side of his head and pulling him to look at me.

"Hey, baby," I say and then kiss him.

"What the hell?" I hear Stella say, but everything else is a blur as Enzo's hand slides into my hair as he twists us around and presses me into the wall with his body as he kisses me harder. His lips devour my own as I slide my hands into his hair, and he groans.

"Miss Crowe?" I hear my name being shouted from down the corridor.

"You've got to be fucking kidding me," Enzo mutters against my lips. He pulls away, and we turn to face Mr. Daniels.

"Seeing as you've finished so early, we can squeeze in another training session. Training room, fifteen minutes," he says, and then turns to head back down the corridor. My stomach growls as if in protest. *Fuck's sake.*

"Come on, let's quickly grab you a sandwich or something before he throws you on your ass," Enzo offers, tugging me along the corridor in the opposite direction, without waiting for my answer. I turn back and see a calculating look on Stella's face as she looks between Mr. Daniels, Enzo, and me. I shudder, feeling a chill roll through my body. I turn back and walk with Enzo. Time to eat as much food as humanly possible in ten minutes, I suppose.

Chapter 33

KENZIE

*T*he dim lighting in the room does nothing to hide the predatory look on his face as he stalks around me, moving in a circle. I keep trying to move with him, to keep my eyes on him and my back away, but he's just too quick. He shoots flames to my left, and I jump to my right, narrowly avoiding the hit.

I try to counter with air, calling on my mark. I aim low, hoping to strike him off balance. He blocks my attack with a simple swipe of his hand. A cool jet of water flows from his right hand, he doesn't aim it at me, but at the floor. I stare at him in confusion, when suddenly the water begins to cool and freeze over. I struggle not to slide across it. I lift my left hand and command fire, using fire's heat to melt the ice. The steam creates a wall between us. I try to use it as a screen to attack, but he simply uses his air ability to clear his vision again. I back up a few steps to keep out of reach, but he pounces, crossing the space between us. Within seconds I'm pinned down onto the blue mat by his weight. I struggle to get loose, completely forgetting to use my magic in order to assist me.

"Miss Crowe," he whispers in my ear softly, his deep voice sending shivers right through me.

"Kenzie," I mumble.

"What?" he asks.

"Please call me Kenzie," I whisper.

"Miss Kenzie Crowe," he utters softly, his cool breath against my neck making me shiver.

"Yes?" I whisper, looking up, I catch the heated look in his green eyes.

"You would be dead six times over if I was really trying."

I laugh, but it's a somewhat strangled sound. I look away from his heated stare, cutting off the temptation, at least, as much as possible while he's all over me. My thoughts about Mr. Daniels are going to kill me.

I wriggle slightly, trying to see if there is any chance of getting him off me without the use of magic. No dice. I think about his advice. Don't use magic the way they expect you to. Surprising them is half the battle, blah, blah, blah. Yeah, that's pretty exact I'm sure. The 'blah blahs' is *definitely* how his speech ended.

A stroke of genius hits me, and a smile takes over my face.

"What are you thinking, Miss Crowe?" he asks softly.

"Nothing," the word flies out of my mouth, and I'm sure I look guilty. I concentrate, while attempting to look like I am not concentrating, which is apparently ridiculously hard to pull off, as I feel his body vibrating with laughter above me. I call on my technomancy mark.

The lights start to flicker above us.

"Flickering lights, really?" he questions, the amusement thick in his voice.

I cut the lights off completely and scream, as I use my transmutation to change my eyes into a wolf's eyes. *Night vision, I impress myself sometimes.*

"Shit, was that not you?" he asks. I use the moment of concern against him, and twist out from underneath him, blasting him with air to help me with just the lift needed to escape.

In the darkness, I have the upper hand.

I use my water ability to use his own tricks against him, covering the whole floor in ice. I kick my shoes off, and heat my feet with my fire, so I can move effectively around without slipping.

I stalk around him in a circle, now he is the prey, and I'm the predator. I launch at him, feeling the animal-like dexterity in me aid my attack. He dodges at the last possible moment, and jabs a fist into my side. *Fuck!*

I back up a few paces and circle him again. *Shit, how did he know I was there?*

"Move lighter on your feet, Miss Crowe," he says softly. *Is he a freaking mind reader? Is it a secret bonus ability or something?* I try to move quieter. "Better," he says.

He lashes out and grabs hold of me, pulling me to him, before spinning us around and planting me against the wall. "But, not good enough," he murmurs into my ear. The tone in his voice is so seductive, I swear it *has to* be on purpose.

I lick my lips, seeing as they feel so suddenly dry. *I'm so freaking stupid, he's so unbelievably perfect, and here I am just fawning over him. Idiot.*

"Excuse me, Miss Crowe?"

"Did I say that out loud? Wait how much of that did I just say out loud?"

"Just the word 'idiot'. Why, what else were you thinking?" his body seems to move even closer up to mine. *Fuck.*

"N-nothing," I stumble the word out.

"It doesn't seem like nothing. You wouldn't be lying to me, would you, Kenzie?" the way he says my first name, as if on an exhale of breath. *Shit, bad thoughts; bad, bad thoughts.* "Kenzie?" he repeats, softly.

I tilt my head up, seeing him perfectly in the dark thanks to my wolf eyesight. I focus and bring my eyes back to normal. If I see him, I won't be able to do this. With my eyes back to normal, I can't see him at all, but I know exactly where he is. I lean up, closing the gap between us, and press my lips against his.

At first, nothing. He seems too stunned to react, I'm about to pull back and apologise for completely misreading the situation, when he returns the kiss, a satisfied groan coming from him when I push myself up closer against him. His hand snakes into my hair, pulling it from the ponytail and letting it down. I move my hands up his shirt, feeling across the hard planes of his chest. He bites my bottom lip, and I moan softly, opening my mouth and deepening the kiss. He seems to come undone, tugging at my shirt, it comes off, his follows straight after it. It seems like a desperate rush on both our parts. The tension of the past few weeks finally getting to us. It can't be ignored anymore. *I need this, right now.*

I go for his jogging bottoms, sliding them down his toned legs. He lifts me up, and pins me against the wall. I wrap my legs around him, feeling him pressed right up against me. He presses a kiss against my neck, before biting down. *Fuck I need out of my leggings, right now.* I reach a hand down to start to pull them off, when light shines into the room from the door. The now open door. *Fuck.*

He springs back from me, and we stare at the light from the door like deer in headlights. The collision tumbling closer and closer, but we can't look away as we're frozen in place. I can't see the face of the person, but I'd know that body anywhere.

"East, it's not —"

"What it looks like? I think it's exactly what it looks like!" he snaps, cutting my words off. He turns back away from the room.

"Easton!" I call after him. I grab my shirt, pulling it over my head as I race after him. He shuts the door after him.

I pull it open, and dart out into the hall, I look

around, but he has already darted away. *Fuck*. Without a backwards glance at Mr. Daniels, I run off in what I hope is the direction East left in, knowing I can't let him run off after seeing that. Especially not after our conversation this morning damn it! I spot him sitting on the bottom step of the stairs, with people walking past him as they rush to their classes. He looks up at me as I walk over, stopping in front of him.

"East–" I start to say, but stop, not knowing what to say. I'm not sorry for what happened between me and Mr. Daniels, but I'm sorry I didn't tell East how I was feeling about him.

"I don't care that you like him, Kenz, I care that you didn't tell me. I thought . . . well, I thought you would tell me first before you sleep with someone else," he says gently. I expected him to be angry at me, not this, this is worse because I feel guilty.

"I haven't slept with him, and that just happened," I explained and he nods, standing up and coming over to me.

"I mean, after this morning I just . . . I guess I just need some time to think, Kenz," he replies and walks around me. Turning around as I follow him with my eyes, watching him walk down the corridor, feeling like my heart is hurting more with every step he takes away from me.

Chapter 34

KENZIE

"Stupid, damn phone," I mutter as I try to turn the thing on as I walk through the woods and back to the cabin after my lessons. It's getting darker every day, and I can barely see where I'm going. I groan and slide it into my back pocket, knowing I'm more frustrated about everything else in my life than my phone. Enzo is avoiding me since the kiss in the hallway. I haven't seen Mr. Daniels since we got hot and heavy in training, yesterday. East is still mad at me. Ryan is an accomplice in a murder, and I won't speak to Kelly until she apologises for lying to me. The twins are the only ones who aren't annoyed at me, but I haven't seen them much since what happened yesterday with Mr. Daniels. I have the feeling East told them, by the awkward looks I got over the breakfast table this morning.

"Kennie," my brother's voice says from the

shadows of the trees to the right of me, and I nearly jump out of my skin.

"Ryan, what the hell?" I ask, watching as he steps into the moonlight, followed by the rebel girl I saw before and an older man. It doesn't shock me like it should to see them all together, but there's still a sting that my brother would betray me like this. No matter what Kelly says, he is betraying me.

"Kennie, I need you to come with me," he says, using the stupid, childhood nickname and making my heart hurt as I look him over. Ryan has dark hair that is cut short, with a slight beard, and a massive build from the training I know he does. He is paler than I am, but we look so similar. Other than his eyes, which are green compared to my blue.

"Why? Are you working with the rebels as well as fucking my best friend?" I ask, and he flinches ever so slightly. I'm sure Kelly told him I knew, but now, I'm thankful I didn't tell her about hearing any more of their conversation.

"We should just knock her out, we don't need to ask," the girl next to Ryan says, and I watch as he glares down at her.

"No. He said I could do this my way, and this is my way. She will come with us when she understands," Ryan practically growls at the girl, and I take a step back, his eyes turning to watch me as a branch cracks under my shoes.

"Don't run, there are twenty rebels around you, Kennie. Let me explain," he tells me, but I watch the other guy he was with move closer, and he's smiling at me in a creepy way, just as I notice the rope he has in his hands.

"Explain what? Explain that you and Kelly are working for the rebels? That you want to kidnap me? I already know," I spit out, and Ryan shakes his head.

"It's not like that. Kelly didn't—" I cut him off by taking another step and imagining my fire mark. I need to make a big fire and hopefully someone will see it. If I can mix fire and air, setting the trees on fire should work.

"She did, and is just as bad as you. Who killed Mr. Layan? Who was it that you helped dump his body at the bottom of those stairs?" I ask, and he looks shocked for a second.

"Enough of this, we don't have time," the girl says and steps forward just as I call my fire mark. I don't want to hurt Ryan, but this is bigger than my love for my brother. I can't just let him be stupid and get myself kidnapped. I lift my hands and imagine the giant fireball, and then call my air mark like I did on the first day. The effect is instant with the fire and air mixing together. I watch as three massive fire tornados swirl towards my brother and his friends. Ryan's eyes meet mine in a brief gap between the fire, and he shakes his head at me like he is disappointed in me before calling his water mark and making a wall of water in front of him. It's almost ironic, because that's how I feel about him. I don't think about it anymore as I turn and run towards the school, my heart pounding against my chest when I look around. I can't see anyone else, so I'm hoping Ryan was bluffing.

"Run, little marked, I like to play catch," I hear the girl laugh behind me, her voice sounding close. I turn and regret it when I see her inches away from me, and I scream as she hits me with her air mark, sending me flying into a tree and smacking my side against it. I call my protection mark, holding up my hands and imagining the shield as she walks over. When she laughs, I place my hand on the ground calling my water mark and imagining ice. She slips, not expecting it, giving me the second I need to stand up. I freeze her to the ground before I walk a few steps back and place both of my hands on the ground, calling my earth mark. I'm lucky she doesn't have the fire mark, as she struggles to get out of the ice. I imagine the ground opening, praying my earth mark will respond to me now. I watch as she sinks into a deep hole I create, hearing her scream. I walk over, looking down at her in the hole, seeing that she is knocked out. I turn and run.

Breathing a sigh of relief when I see the academy, I slow down slightly, but there is no one around like I expected there to be. I don't stop running completely, knowing I'll be safer inside.

"Stop," a voice calls from behind me, just before I can get to the back doors of the school. I turn around, seeing a man I've seen so many times before in photos around my family home.

But, he's meant to be dead.

"Aren't you going to stop and say hello to your father, Mackenzie?" he questions.

I look into the eyes of my mum's dead husband.

The one that died when I was a baby. The one she mourns every day, and a man that could very well be my father with his black hair and tanned skin. I go to reply when I feel something hard slam against the side of my head and feel myself falling. The last thing I see is my brother running over to me as he shouts something, before everything goes black.

The End...for now...

The story continues in book two, Marked by Pain

Coming February 2018

About the Authors
CECE ROSE

Cece Rose is the proud owner of one dog, four turtles, and one annoying boyfriend.
She hails from Devon in the South-West of England but dreams of sunny skies and sand between her toes. Although, whenever abroad, she will moan about the heat and the sand that gets everywhere.
She has largely convinced all who know her that she is a vampire, mainly due to her nocturnal habits. In reality, it's because her creativity only ever strikes when the sky is dark, and the stars are shining. (Plus, it's actually quiet enough to concentrate on writing.)
You can find Cece on Facebook and Twitter. **And, don't forget to join her Demon Den!**

About the Authors

G. BAILEY

G. Bailey lives in rainy (sometimes sunny) England with her husband, two children, one slightly strange cat.(and now a dog)
When she isn't writing (which is unusual), she can be found reading one of the many books in her house or talking to her amazing readers.
She has a slight addiction to Ben & Jerry's ice cream and chocolate.
Please feel free to stalk her, in her group, Bailey's Pack.

Facebook---Twitter---Website

Other Titles by Cece Rose

THE DESDEMONA CHRONICLES

A Demon's Blade – Released: May 2017

A Demon's Debt – Coming: December 2017

FATED SERIAL

Fractured Fate – Released: July 2017

Twisted Fate – Released: August 2017

Rejecting Fate – Released: September 2017

Accepting Fate – Coming soon

Choosing Fate – Coming soon

VENGEANCE – Coming: December 2017

SNOWFLAKE – Coming: November 2017 (A part of the Snow & Seduction Reverse-Harem anthology.)

Other Titles by G. Bailey

THE KING BROTHERS SERIES

Izzy's Beginning – Released May 2017

Sebastian's Chance – Released May 2017

Elliot's Secret – Released August 2017

Harley's Fall – Coming: January 2018

Luke's Revenge – Coming: March 2018

HER GUARDIAN SERIES

Winter's Guardian – Released June 2017

Winter's Kiss – Released September 2017

Winter's Promise – Released September 2017

Winter's War – Coming: December 2017

SAVED BY PIRATES SERIES

Escape the Sea- Released October 2017

Love the Sea- Coming: January 2018

STRIP FOR ME SERIAL

Part One- Released October 2017

Omnibus with spin off – Released November 2017

Made in the USA
Columbia, SC
06 May 2024

35352337R00157